The Candle Star

Divided Decade Collection

Michelle Isenhoff

Edited by Amy Nemecek.
Cover design by Dale Pease of Walking Stick Books.
All rights reserved.

Lexile score: 800L

ISBN-13: 978-1497450257

Candle Star Press
www.michelleisenhoff.com

For Emily

Chapter One

Detroit, 1858

Emily Preston threatened to hate every moment of her holiday, but sometimes curiosity overcomes even the best of bad intentions. She had to relax her indifference, just for a moment. Palms pressed flat against the cool pane of glass, her blue eyes drank in the sea of buildings whizzing past.

Detroit surprised her. She was certain she'd find a shambling frontier town, but the city was studded with hundreds of tall, flat-topped buildings that looked as if they'd been nailed into the ground by a giant hammer and abandoned at different heights. Wide avenues rolled with respectable folk carried along in every possible kind of horse-drawn conveyance, their clatter muffled by the window. And as the train circled the city, Emily counted no fewer than twelve church spires.

Of course the town wasn't as gracious as Charleston, back home in Carolina, with its stately old homes and picturesque harbor, but a yearling colt could hardly be compared with the noble lines of a full-grown stallion. Detroit had its own charm, a rough and vital energy that Emily could have found invigorating.

If she hadn't been banished here.

5

"Miss Emily, it's not proper, you squashin' yo' nose agains' dat glass."

Emily turned to the old black man with a haughty shrug. "It really doesn't matter how I behave, Zeke. I don't know anyone in this entire state."

"Yo' uncle be waitin' fo' you at de station, miss. You makes a good firs' impression."

"My uncle," she snorted. "He's lived here so long he's probably as dull as the rest of these Yankees." She raised her voice, stretching out each syllable like a string of maple syrup. "We're practically on the frontier. Michigan's only been in the Union for sixteen years. Why, I'm nearly as old as the state."

She tossed her curls, pleased with the dark glances she was generating.

The old man gave her a stern look. "You's thirteen yeahs ol', miss, not sixteen, and you minds yo' mannahs."

"Oh, Ezekiel," she pouted, "if my uncle dislikes me, maybe he'll send me home."

She'd never been away from Ella Wood before, and leaving the beautiful plantation had perforated her heart with a thousand holes, like the side of the smokehouse her brother had riddled with buckshot. Her joy had gushed out all at once, and her confidence, so thick at home, was slowly seeping out and dripping off her toes with every step north.

She missed Ella Wood. She missed the lazy fields dotted with Thoroughbreds swishing their tails and grazing hock-deep in clover. She missed the shady smell of the forest that sprawled so thickly across the hills one nearly stepped on the game sheltered in its tangles. She missed the spectrum of the sunset above the rice fields, turning them russet, then purple, then black. She missed the liquid sound of music flowing from the slave cabins after dusk.

But that was all a million miles behind her now, lost in

6

a moment of high spirits—a tantrum, her mother called it—that convinced her parents she needed a change of scenery and a firmer hand. So she'd been packed up and sent to her mother's brother in Detroit.

They didn't tell her the North was practically a different country, one that dispensed frowns of disapproval for traveling with an old slave. Nor did they mention the discomforts of railroad travel, the tasteless food, the terrible service. She'd just been tossed over the Mason-Dixon Line like a rabbit pitched into a kennel of hounds.

The track rounded a final bend and ended beside a busy waterfront littered with crates and barrels and coarse-looking dockhands. A score of ships lined the river, scratching heaven's floorboards with their bobbing masts, waiting to take aboard the raw timber that rose up in towers beside the tracks.

Emily watched a dog dodge beneath a team of drays that stood ready to haul away the cargo being unloaded from a slumbering steamship. Beyond lay the murky green of the Detroit River, then the emerald plain of Canada.

The train shuddered and died, wheezing out a last breath of steam. Moments later, passengers poured from its belly, covering the platform like a brightly knitted afghan before ducking into the depot with its cinnamon-colored bricks.

"You keeps out o' trouble till I fines our luggage, Miss Emily," Zeke admonished as he joined the throng.

Emily remained seated until the crush in the aisle disappeared. Through the window, she watched the whirl of people mixing and merging and sorting themselves out. Loved ones called to each other and embraced, and in the most crowded moment she felt a powerful sting of loneliness. But she adjusted her hat, securing both the headpiece and her courage, and stepped off the train.

The yard reeked of grease, coal smoke, horse manure

and fish, but she eagerly stretched her legs. From some distance on the river, the whistle of a steamship warbled in the breeze. All around her, the city throbbed with its own importance. Conversations flitted about like barn swallows, and a busy clop-clop testified to daily commerce taking place beyond the depot. Overhead, the sky shone as blue as the eyes of the china doll on her bed at home, and the cheery autumn sun poured down gold at her feet in welcome.

A hatless man approached dressed in a cheap, brown suit. It was unbuttoned and flapped in the breeze he created as he strode toward her. His necktie was skewed, and his forehead spilled over with a riot of dark curls that he brushed at absently and ineffectually. "Emily Preston," he hailed.

She eyed him distastefully. Had her uncle sent this buffoon to meet her?

"Yes, I am Miss Preston," she answered curtly.

Amusement hinted in the crinkle of his eyes. "Oh, it wasn't a question. You're the only Southern belle on the platform. And a Milford through and through, I'll add."

Irritating Yank. She pulled herself up to her full height and gave him a scathing look. "Manners die out north of Richmond, I've noticed."

The man bent in a sweeping bow. "Miss Preston," he said, smiling openly now, "I'm pleased to meet you. I'm your uncle, Isaac Milford."

She gaped at him. "You can't be!"

He threw back his head and laughed. "I assure you, I can. Were you expecting someone else?"

She bristled. "I was expecting someone more like my mother."

"Ah," he replied with a lift of his eyebrows. "Someone refined and gentle and polite. I'm sorry to disappoint you, but my sister and I inherited very few of the same qualities.

8

You'll have to settle for blunt, tactless and stubborn. Thoroughly insufferable, I'm afraid."

Perfect. At least he fit nicely into the theme of her trip.

Ezekiel approached just then carrying her carpetbag and his own small valise. Two sturdy railroad workers trailed behind him bearing her iron-bound steamer trunk between them.

Isaac thumped the black man heartily on the back. "Zeke, it's good to see you. How long has it been, fifteen years?"

The old slave grinned, revealing his few remaining teeth. "Long about dat, I 'spects. Marse Isaac, you sho' looks fine all growed up."

Isaac chuckled. "Perhaps, considering the loose-kneed, gangly kid you remember. Well, come along, you two. My rig is parked out front."

The "rig" was a large, open carriage. Harnessed before it stood two hacks of indeterminate breeding, one gray, one sorrel. The workers hefted the trunk onto the vehicle's rear-facing seat, and Emily and Zeke settled across from it.

Isaac climbed onto the driver's bench. "All set?"

Taking her shrug as an affirmative, he flicked the reins over the backs of the mismatched team. Emily vowed disinterest, but when the huge mills and dockside warehouses merged into rows of storefronts aproned in brightly colored awnings, her traitorous curiosity got the best of her again.

They jogged around a corner and found themselves in the middle of an outdoor marketplace. The road broadened to twice its normal width, and in its center stood two long, low, open-air structures filled with vendors and their wares. In one glance, Emily took in a load of golden squash, a wagon displaying needlework and home-canned produce, a crate of squawking hens, and three barrels of apples, each of a different color.

"This is Central Market," Isaac informed them. "Michigan Avenue runs straight out to the countryside. Makes it convenient for the farmers to haul their goods to town."

Next, they turned onto a wide avenue hedged with storefronts. Some of the buildings rose up five or six stories, with giant letters between each row of windows spelling out their business. Others boasted only two or three floors, with living quarters on the uppermost and gabled peaks above. All stood with shoulders crammed together so tightly a hand couldn't have passed between them.

"We're almost home," Isaac called out, rounding one last corner.

Moments later they pulled up in front of an old brick house skirted with a gray porch and set back from the road. A row of brilliant mums grew before it like lace edging on the bottom hem of a dress. In the exact center of the building's face sat a red door, with two windows on either side and matching windows above. The gravel drive curved into the backyard, and the front lawn boasted a sign with "River Street Inn" painted in letters as curly as the locks on her uncle's forehead.

Emily read the sign a second time. A hotel? Her uncle lived in a hotel? How had her parents forgotten to mention this tiny detail?

Isaac must have read her confusion. He explained with some pride, "This used to be a private residence, but I remodeled it into an inn. It earns me a decent living." He offered Emily a hand down. "I hope you will consider it your home during your stay. It's no Russell House, but there are those who've said it's comfortable."

Emily scanned the building with keen disapproval, like a judge about to sentence a felon. "I suppose it would do if one was used to primitive accommodations."

Her uncle seemed to struggle with a twitch that pulled up one corner of his mouth. "I'm glad you're here, Emily.

10

I've been looking forward to this opportunity to get to know my only niece."

And that's when her plan formed. The idea had nudged her on the train, but only now did she see the possibilities. She would make him regret that he had ever met her. She'd make herself so obnoxious and hateful that he wouldn't be able to endure her—and he would send her home!

Chapter Two

"I'm really very tired," Emily said curtly. "I'd like to be shown to my room."

"Of course." Isaac opened the front door. In a glance, she took in a spacious lobby with several chairs scattered across a floral carpet. A wide fireplace climbed the wall between two windows on her left, and to the right sprawled a large desk where hotel business was conducted. An office was visible behind it through the open top of a Dutch door.

Just past the desk, her uncle led her through a second door that opened into a short hallway with four rooms set opposite each other. "These are my private quarters. This is another door to my office; my bedroom is beyond. You'll be across from me, with Zeke next to you. The rooms aren't large, but no guests will disturb you.

"I'll bring your trunk in as soon as I can round up some help," he offered, ushering her into the bedroom. "Settle in and rest. Dinner is served at five o'clock. Tonight we'll take it with the guests."

He closed the door firmly, and Emily was left alone.

She stood in the center of the room and spun in a slow circle. It was about as accommodating as a woodshed—nothing like her luxurious bedroom at Ella Wood. Just a wardrobe, a desk, a table with bowl and pitcher, a chipped chamber pot, and a bed draped with a quilt as dingy and faded as death. The only color in the whole room came from an ugly rag rug pitched onto the floor.

A knock interrupted her survey. "Miss Emily, I has yo' bag."

"Bring it in please, Zeke."

He entered as gently as a lamb and placed it on the bed. "Does you need anything else, miss? This ol' back sho' could use some rest aftah dat rattlin' train ride."

"I'm fine, Zeke. Go lie down."

He nodded, easing the door closed behind him.

Emily sat and pulled the bag onto her lap. Rummaging inside, she drew out a book of poetry her mother had given her at the train station. With a grimace, she shoved the volume to the bottom of the bag, exchanging it for a penny novel smuggled to her by her best friend, Sophia. This she slid beneath her pillow. Reaching in again, she located a small watercolor of Ella Wood painted in springtime bloom. It was her best work yet, and she displayed it on the desk to remind her of home. Finally she pulled out her paints and a tablet of thick paper and stored them in a desk drawer.

With nothing left to occupy her, Emily flopped back against the shroud of a quilt and watched the light reflect off the water in the pitcher and frolic on the ceiling. But like a ghost that wouldn't stay dead, her indomitable curiosity rose up inside her. She wrestled with it only a moment before slipping from the room.

Zeke's snoring filled the hall with a soft rhythm, like gentle waves sighing against the sand of Charleston Neck. With a furtive glance, Emily tried the knob of her uncle's bedroom door. It opened silently, revealing a room identical to her own. With a snort of disdain, she closed it and moved on to his office, hoping for something—anything—amusing, but the knob wouldn't budge. She'd try again later.

She entered the vacant lobby. An open stairway spilled from the second story, partitioning off a dining area in the back set with eight round tables. Emily was drawn to a pair of French doors that brightened the room and overlooked a sizable garden at the rear of the hotel. Her stomach rumbled as she walked into the aroma of baking bread.

"No, I ain't seen her yet, an' I's in no hurry to."

Emily froze. The muffled words drifted from behind the wall, accompanied by the clanking of dishes.

"Oh, Julia, you have everyone from the South stuffed in the same sack." This woman sounded younger, and her voice rolled with a foreign accent.

"I knows what I knows," Julia stubbornly maintained.

"Well, I'm impatient to meet her. I have seven nieces and nephews of my own, and I enjoy them so much. I'm eager to adopt Isaac's as well."

They were talking about her, Emily realized. She pressed her ear to the kitchen door.

"I hope you's right, Shannon," but the voice didn't sound like it held out any hope at all.

A clatter of pans met Emily's ear, and then, "We're almost out of stove wood. Should I call Malachi?"

"He out fishin' wid dat Willis boy. Mr. Isaac gib him de afternoon off."

"Then I'll tell him when he gets back. Do you have a bowl? I think these potatoes are done."

Emily lost interest in the conversation. In fact, nothing in her new prison seemed to draw her interest except, perhaps, the lure of the still-unexplored second story. But a quick peek through the keyholes upstairs revealed eight more rooms remarkable only in their plainness.

That was it? This was where she had to live until her parents chose to bring her home? With a clown of an uncle, some woman who already hated her, and another who wanted to make her a pet?

She leaned weakly against the last doorframe in the corridor. She'd best start working on that escape plan right away!

She was distracted by delicate strains of piano music sifting up through the floorboards and settling on her like fine powder. With a start, she recognized the sonata as one of her mother's favorites. How strange to hear it played so far from home. And how welcome! Could she dare hope that her uncle had hired dinner music?

Emily crept down the stairway and peered over the banister. She had not noticed it as she passed through the lobby, but there, pushed up against the stairway wall, stood a small upright piano. And to her utter astonishment, it was her uncle who sat before the instrument coaxing out music as sweet as brown sugar! She listened, spellbound.

Isaac moved smoothly into one of Bach's minuets and then to a pair of hymns. Emily sank to the steps and closed her eyes, the familiar melodies conjuring up pictures of home. When her uncle changed to the haunting strains of Beethoven's "Moonlight Sonata," she could picture her mother seated before her beloved baby grand, hands skimming the keys, body rocking with the intensity of her playing.

Emily's heart wrenched with a twist of homesickness. When the music slowed and faded away, she sat immobile, saturated in memories that threatened to leak out and roll down her cheeks.

A round of applause erupted below. "What a beautiful performance, Mr. Milford! I didn't know thee played."

Isaac spun on the seat. "Mrs. Bronner! I didn't hear you come in." He addressed an elderly woman perched on the divan behind him.

"Of course thee didn't. I wouldn't interrupt such fine talent."

Isaac gave her a quizzical look. "I thought Quakers

15

considered music vanity."

"Oh, we do!" She dropped her voice conspiratorially. "But I was raised Methodist."

Isaac chuckled and stood as the front door opened. "Good afternoon, Mr. Bronner," he said with a nod. "Were you able to find another retailer for your furniture?"

A gray-haired man dressed all in black gave her uncle a dignified nod. "I received orders for three more rocking chairs and a bureau. Enough to keep me busy for several weeks."

"And I enjoyed a lovely tour of the city," chimed Mrs. Bronner.

Isaac smiled. "Then your visit has been a complete success. Forgive my poor manners, but I have a few things I must attend to. Will I see you both at dinner?" At their nods, he closed himself behind the Dutch door.

As soon as it latched, Emily fled past the astonished couple and out the garden doors, sucking in deep breaths of air to keep her emotions in check. But it was like holding a litter of puppies inside a shallow basket. A few tears managed to escape. She wiped at them angrily. She would not cry! Instead, she'd channel that energy and use it to get what she wanted.

She found herself on a flagstone patio. Though in the midst of a crowded city, the house had managed to retain a bit of space around itself, like legroom granted to a tottering old man. The entire backyard was laid out in the geometrical shapes of a French garden and enclosed by a high brick wall. Emily could smell the green scent of growing things, made sharper by the coolness of early autumn. She entered, following a path of crushed limestone.

The path wound through the different garden rooms, each bordered with clipped, shoulder-high hedges and planted with a unique theme. The first boasted vibrantly hued asters, zinnias, and daisies all leaning heavily against

16

each other on tall, slender stalks. The next held only herbs, low-growing and fragrant. Another grew blooms all ghostly white, winding into the hedge and surrounding a pair of white wicker benches. Yet another displayed formal tea roses in every color, complete with a wrought iron table and matching chairs.

The garden was too perfect for Emily's tastes. Too tame. Too forced and manipulated. All these plants were compelled to follow some gardener's wishes instead of growing free and unhindered. As she strolled down the path, she identified with them, for the same constrictions had recently been imposed on her.

For twelve years Emily Preston had been indulged and allowed to ramble at will, carefree and happy. Suddenly her parents realized she would be marriageable in only a few short years and began to prepare her. They controlled and contained her—just like the plants being forced into these boxes. All the new rules made her want to run, to scream, to fly away! How could she be held accountable for her sudden bursts of temper?

Emily entered the garden's very last room. Unlike the others, this one was choked with weeds. They grew in random disarray, intertwining and bulging over the path. Emily's heart lightened as she identified many of the same wildflowers that grew in the fields of Ella Wood: Indian paintbrush, blue chicory, black-eyed Susan, and the flat, feathery bloom of the yarrow. She scooped up handfuls to brighten her room.

The path emerged near a stable at the back of the lot. Peering inside, she saw that five of the stalls were occupied. She recognized her uncle's team at once. A name plate nailed over the gray's head gave its name Barnabas; the sorrel was called Mabel. The stable also housed a pair of matched bays and a beautiful black riding mare.

Emily was drawn to the mare. Its small ears were

pricked forward, and it watched her with intelligent eyes. As she rubbed its forehead, Emily wished she had a carrot in her pocket. Instead, she offered it a clover blossom. The horse was quite valuable and reminded her of Chantilly, her own saddle mare. Did it belong to a guest, or could her uncle own such a fine animal?

Her attention shifted to the door of the very last stall. It was closed, but no head showed over the top. Instead, odd snuffling sounds issued from within. Her curiosity aroused, she peered inside. At the same moment, something rose up in an explosion of noise and brown fur.

Screaming, Emily stumbled backwards and landed on her backside in an empty stall, flowers strewn everywhere. A huge, rangy hound stood with paws hooked over the top of the stall door, staring down at her with head tilted and floppy ears cocked as if it couldn't quite figure out what she was. It bayed again, long and throaty, and dropped back inside the stall.

"Stupid mutt!" she yelled, flinging a clod of mud that struck the door and disintegrated into a puff of gray powder. She brushed straw and petals off her dress and gave the dog's door a swift kick. A second hound appeared, bawling out another long, wailing bellow.

She lurched backward and snatched up her bouquet. Keeping a wary eye on the half-door, she stormed toward the exit.

At the door she hesitated, a devilish look narrowing her eyes and tightening her lips. She waited till the dogs settled down before she crept back to their stall and scattered her flowers before it once again. Then she turned the latch until it barely held. If the dogs pounced on it even once, the door would fling open and they would be free. And with any luck, the flowers would point to her.

With a devious chuckle, Emily hustled up the gravel lane to the front of the house, hoping the mongrels didn't

18

gain their freedom until she reached safety. She paused only briefly to pick half a dozen mums from the porch's flower border before entering.

It must have been nearly time for dinner, but as she passed her uncle's office she slowed. She would dearly love a look inside his private room. Surely, she could turn up some morsel of information to twist to her own uses.

She pressed her ear to the door. All was quiet. Glancing up and down the deserted hallway, she tried the knob again.

This time it turned.

She slipped inside, quiet as a falling leaf, and closed the door behind her.

Like the bedrooms, the office was plain, almost stark. Aside from a desk, a chair, and a small shelf of books, the only other furnishing in the room was an oil painting of a magnolia tree in full bloom. In the corner, looking extremely out of place, were stacked five shiny tin buckets with half a dozen hammers placed in the topmost one.

Emily moved to the bookshelf and glanced through the titles: *Pilgrim's Progress*, *A History of the Great Lakes Region*, *Selected Sermons of George Whitefield*, *A Complete Guide to Managing Business Finance*, and a collection of poems by Henry Wadsworth Longfellow. Her breath escaped in a long whisper of disbelief. Did her uncle actually read this stuff?

She set down her flowers and bent over the desk. In contrast to the tidy room, it looked like a dynamited paper factory. Poking through the mess, she pulled out several handwritten receipts, a clipping from a newspaper advertising railroad stock, pages ripped from a ledger, a shopping list, and stacks of hotel business. A pried-up handful revealed only more of the same underneath.

She dropped the papers in disgust and tried a drawer. Each was filled with the same papery clutter. She recalled her father's neatly organized desk at home. How could her uncle run a business this way?

Disappointed, she gathered the mums. The break-in had gained her nothing. But as she turned away, something caught her eye. Something that wasn't quite right.

A gap appeared where two panels of the desk came together. She bent closer and ran a finger over the opening. It was a secret compartment. One that would be completely hidden beneath the writing surface of the desk if only her uncle had closed it properly. But thanks to his carelessness, she had discovered it!

She reached her fingers into the space and pulled out a brown, leather-bound volume with a star embossed on its cover. With a furtive glance at the door, she opened the book.

It was some kind of journal. She could tell by the dates written in the margins, but the entries made no sense at all. They appeared to be simple lists; food, clothing, objects, names, places, and money amounts. Nor had it been written in every day. Not even every week. Thumbing backward, she saw seven entries for July, two in June, several in May, then nothing till March, and only one in January. Flipping back farther, she saw the journal ran for years. What could it mean?

Glancing up at the clock on the bookshelf, she saw it read 4:40. She had just enough time to dress for dinner. Vowing to give the book more thought later, she slid it back into its hiding place, closed the compartment firmly, and slipped into the hall.

Chapter Three

Back in her room, Emily was pleased to find her trunk on the floor at the foot of her bed. She dropped the mums into the pitcher of water and splayed out the skirt of her traveling suit. It was stained, wrinkled, and smeared with muck from the stable—not at all suitable for dinner. She couldn't abide the thought of any Yankees looking down their nose at her.

She opened the trunk and pulled out a beautiful gray taffeta dress with sleeves as wide as bells and dripping with lace. Layer upon layer of ruffles made up the skirt, which flounced wide over a crinoline petticoat and a pair of frilly pantalettes and fell several inches below her knees.

It was the most expensive dress Emily owned, the one her father had ordered special from Paris. But how was she to get it on by herself? Her maid, Lizzie, always assisted her, draping the gown carefully over her head, fastening buttons, tying bows just right, and pinning her curls. Lizzie, however, was young and willful and had been forbidden from making the trip with her. Emily's parents were afraid Lizzie would run away in the free North; old, reliable Zeke had been sent instead. But what good was a doddering old man when dressing for dinner?

Emily wriggled out of the traveling suit with some

trouble and stepped into the undergarments. Getting the elaborate dress over her head proved much more difficult, but with a few grunts and a lot of willpower, it finally settled in place. She did her best to tie a proper bow behind her back, but it looked sadly wilted, like a vase full of daisies too long without water. Nothing like the crisp, perfect knot Lizzie always tied.

She moved on to her hair, glancing into her hand mirror with dismay. Her curls had pulled free of their combs and straggled in wild disarray. She reached for her brush, pulling it through the locks with long, unpracticed strokes, but her hair lay limp and dirty on her shoulders.

At home, she wouldn't have given any more thought to her appearance than a mule would give to its tail. What did the wind and the woods care how she looked? But here her pride was at stake. And at the moment, that was all she had.

A knock sounded at her door, and a woman called out, "Miss Preston? Isaac sent me to remind you that dinner is in five minutes."

Emily recognized the rolling voice from the kitchen.

"Miss Preston?" The door opened and a young, red-haired woman peeked inside. She was hardly more than a girl. "So you are up. I thought perhaps you fell asleep after your long trip." The woman took in Emily's sloppy appearance. "Oh dear. I believe you could use some help."

She crossed the room uninvited and began tugging and adjusting the gray dress. She corrected a button, pulled the back hem free from where it had tucked under the pantalettes, and retied the bow. Then she reached for the brush and with a few practiced twists fastened the curls in a simple style.

Emily admired the effect in the mirror.

"I'm Shannon, by the way. Shannon Burns. I used to wait on Lady Pennington back in Ireland, but now I clean for Isaac and sometimes help with dinner. I'm very pleased to meet you. I hope we'll be friends."

Emily frowned at the maid's informal overture and the disrespectful use of her uncle's first name, but Shannon didn't seem to notice. Instead, the maid gave the bow one final tug. "Dinner will be waiting," she called as she left the room.

Emily took one last, approving glance in the mirror and adjusted her arrogance. Just let any person in this hotel try to find fault with her now!

In the dining room, several guests were already seated, and Shannon was busy taking orders. As Emily stood near the stairs wondering where to go, a black woman pushed through the swinging kitchen door and delivered two steaming plates of food.

Isaac waved. "Emily, I saved you a place beside me. Come." He pulled out a chair for her. "I've already ordered."

"Breakfast and lunch are served only to guests, but a few nights a week we open our dinner hour to the public," he explained as she scanned the busy room. Five other tables were occupied, including one where Mr. and Mrs. Bronner sat.

Smiling, Shannon brought them each a plate loaded with mashed potatoes, green peas and a thick pork chop. The whole plate was covered with steaming gravy that tickled her nose as she waited for Isaac to finish saying grace. As the prayer went on, his low tones were overpowered by the familiar sound of a Southern voice.

"They just disappeared," it said. "I don't understand it."

Emily's heart leaped! She peeked with one eye to see who had spoken and discovered a young man seated at the next table, neatly dressed and sporting a full beard. His hair was parted on one side and combed in a wave over his forehead. He sat with two friends who appeared rough and

23

unkempt. As she watched, one of them replied, "We'll go south tomorrow, down to the river."

"Amen," Isaac finished and started eating without another word.

Emily took a few small bites but continued to cast glances at the next table until she caught the eye of the well-dressed man. "Excuse me," she broke in, "but I overheard you talking, and it is so good to hear someone from home. I declare, I was beginning to feel all alone in this godforsaken state."

Isaac frowned at her impulsiveness, but the gentleman flashed a gallant smile. "Well, I'll be! A Dixie flower in the middle of Michigan! Isaac, where have you been hiding this delightful child?"

"Good evening, Jarrod," Isaac said with a polite nod at his guest. "This is my niece, Miss Emily Preston, from Charleston, South Carolina. She arrived today. Emily, Mr. Jarrod Burrows, a regular patron of mine."

Mr. Burrows bowed politely across the tables. "It's a pleasure to meet you, Miss Preston. And I know exactly what you mean about leaving civilization for these northern climates. One can get to feeling a bit forlorn."

"Are you from Carolina, Mr. Burrows?" Emily asked.

"No, miss. Virginia born and bred."

"What are you doing so far from home?"

"I run sort of a detective agency, you might say."

One of his companions choked, and the other slapped him heartily on the back. Emily could see the Bronners glancing in their direction.

"How intriguing!" she burst out. "I've never met anyone in your line of work. What are you investigating?"

"Emily, let's allow Mr. Burrows to finish his dinner in peace," her uncle warned.

His reluctance only made her redouble her efforts. She pretended to pout, her mouth puckered like gathers in a skirt, but her eyes danced. The look worked on her father every time. "But I do so want to know what Mr. Burrows is about. I may ask, mayn't I?"

Mr. Burrows smiled, charmed by her childish petulance. "Certainly she may, Isaac." He explained, "A friend of mine back home had a valuable piece of property stolen from him. He has hired me to recover it for him."

The Bronners now stared openly at them. Emily pretended not to notice their lack of etiquette. "How noble of you, Mr. Burrows, but couldn't that get dangerous?"

"A very real possibility. That is why I have brought along my companions, Joseph Sturgis and Edward Satterfield."

Both mumbled a greeting.

Mr. Bronner set down his napkin and cleared his throat. "Would this property have taken flight of its own accord?" he interrupted.

Mr. Burrows chuckled. "That would be something, wouldn't it, sir?"

But the elderly man wasn't put off. Fire snapped in his eyes as they bored into Mr. Burrows. "Property indeed!"

Satterfield leaned back in his chair and picked at his teeth with a dirty fingernail. "That's what the law calls this particular item, and we have every intention of returning it to its rightful owner."

The tension in the room mounted, and Emily searched the face of each speaker. What were they talking about?

Mr. Bronner shifted his gaze to Satterfield. "How, sir, does thee reconcile the law and your Christian faith? The man thee seeks was made in the very image of God."

Satterfield leaned forward threateningly. "God ain't black."

Mr. Burrows stood and offered the elderly couple a conciliatory smile. "I really had no intention of disrupting your meal, and I do apologize. It was tactless of me to discuss business at the dinner table."

"Business!" Mr. Bronner scoffed, also rising. "Son, thee is nothing but a common bounty hunter!"

A sudden gasp escaped Emily's lips. The men were slave catchers!

Mrs. Bronner spoke quietly. "Our nation is founded on the truth that all men are created equal. Yet thee would condemn a man to a life of bondage?"

"It ain't so hard to do, ma'am," Satterfield said, leaning back and exchanging amused grins with Sturgis.

Mr. Bronner seemed gentled by his wife's example. "Forgive me," he said to the men. "I am a man of peace. But I am also a man guided by the Word of the Lord, and I will not break bread with those who seek to enslave another."

Before following her husband from the room, Mrs. Bronner gave them a gentle nod. "I will pray for each of thee tonight."

Sturgis nodded back. "Please do that, ma'am. Maybe we'll catch that darkie and get back to 'Ginnie all the sooner."

Throughout the conflict, the guests at the other tables had fallen silent, eyes downcast, eating with earnest concentration. When the Quaker couple was gone, Mr. Burrows turned to Emily's uncle. "I apologize, Isaac. I didn't mean to drive away customers."

Isaac appeared grave. "Gentlemen, you are always welcome in my establishment, but I must insist that you keep your business to yourselves in the presence of my other guests."

Mr. Burrows nodded shortly. "Agreed."

Emily looked her uncle up and down with disgust. How could he chastise Mr. Burrows? The man had done nothing wrong. Had her uncle been so long in the North that he had forgotten his roots?

26

She, at least, wasn't bound by her uncle's wishes. Turning back to Mr. Burrows, she continued, "I imagine runaways keep you pretty busy. We lost one off our place this year, too."

"Emily," her uncle warned, but she ignored him.

"These Yankees don't understand how things really are. They get all the wrong ideas from that book, *Uncle Tom's Cabin*. They don't realize the Negroes have need of direction and provision."

As she spoke, Ezekiel stood at the side of the room and never fluttered an eyelid, but the black woman who helped serve the meal glared balefully in Emily's direction.

Emily was undaunted. "I hope you catch that fellow. Sometimes the slaves get a little rebellious, like a spirited horse, and they need a firm hand."

Sturgis and Satterfield snorted contemptuously.

"Emily, that will be enough," her uncle commanded.

A sudden baying erupted in the backyard. A glance out the window showed two rangy bloodhounds loping through the carefully manicured garden. They stopped, nosing about in a patch of purple asters. Dirt and blooms began to fly beneath huge paws.

With a muffled oath, the bounty hunters jumped up, stumbling in their haste. Mr. Burrows rose also. "It's been a pleasure," he said with a swift bow. "If you'll excuse me."

The smaller dog still ripped into the flower bed, but the larger one had moved on. It snuffled about the tea roses and stopped to water the hedge as the two men charged out the door. Emily barely stifled a giggle as one of them lunged for its collar.

Isaac stood up from the table and cleared his throat. "Emily, would you accompany me to my office, please?" He wasn't smiling.

"Of course, Uncle," she beamed.

In the office, Isaac closed the door and crossed his

arms in consternation. "It seems you've sufficiently recovered your energy from your trip, my dear. You put on quite a presentation out there. So I believe tomorrow will be soon enough to assign you some chores."

Her smile vanished and her face opened in shock.

"I know your mother has not raised you to be extremely industrious, but I believe a bit of labor is beneficial. So tomorrow you will accompany Shannon."

"You cannot be serious!"

"I assure you, I'm quite serious."

Emily balled her fists at her sides and felt warmth creep into her cheeks. "Uncle Isaac, I am not a slave. And my parents did not send me here to be treated like one. I absolutely refuse to spend my whole day laboring!"

"No, no, you misunderstand," he explained with a lifted eyebrow. "It's just for a while in the evenings. You'll be far too busy attending school to help during the day."

Emily's mouth popped open, and her eyes bulged like a sausage that's been squeezed too hard in the middle.

The corner of her uncle's mouth began to twitch again. "Pick your chin up off the floor, dear. You couldn't possibly have thought I'd hire you a tutor."

Speechless, she whirled to leave, but he stopped her. "One more thing. Jarrod Burrows could charm the stink off a skunk, but I don't want you consorting with him. So no more performances like that last one, please."

She met the command with stony silence, her chin up and her eyes flashing. She would consort with whomever she pleased. When she found her voice it came out strained. "I will be writing home about this," she seethed. Contemptuously, she looked him up and down. "I cannot even fathom how you can be my uncle, you—you Yankee!"

He gave her a grave stare. "Oh, my dear, we are so much more alike than you would ever care to admit."

Chapter Four

Emily stepped daintily over a mud puddle. It had rained overnight, and the streets were an equal mix of gravel, manure, and quicksand. Already her slippers were caked with filth, and mud polka-dotted her pantalettes and the hem of her second best dress. Up the street, she could see the schoolhouse and hear the squeals and laughter of children.

"I still don't understand why we couldn't drive," she complained to her uncle.

"Every other child in this town walks. God gave you two good feet. Use them."

"But I'm not used to walking. My feet are delicate."

"Then I'll buy you a pair of sturdy shoes and a sensible dress to go with them."

At this Emily lifted a haughty chin. "I am the daughter of William and Eleanor Preston, and I will dress like it!" This morning, more than any other morning, it was important that she look her part. Her schoolmates must not notice her trembling knees or guess her uncertainty.

"You may dress like Saint Nicholas for all it matters to me," her uncle stated, "but I will not drive you to school every morning."

He was so unreasonable! She stomped her foot, splashing more mud on herself.

"Look what you've made me do," she wailed, holding the hem of her dress.

Isaac knelt down and wiped at the fabric with his handkerchief. "Sweetheart, you're going to have to try a little harder to fit in around here. I'll help if you'll only give me a chance."

She flung a drop of mud off her face. "I do not need your help."

He rose. "I'll meet you here at noon, just this once, to walk you home for lunch."

"I can find my own way, thank you," she snapped.

"I'll be here."

***

The schoolhouse was a small, one-room wooden structure that looked completely out of place in the city that had grown up around it. It was long and low, with a tiny bell tower on the roof and four windows along each side. The building wasn't quite square anymore, and here and there the paint was flaking where tiny fingers picked at it during recess. The schoolhouse sat on a large lot, apart from its neighbors, looking lonesome, old-fashioned, and much too tired to manage the number of children playing in its yard.

As Emily watched, a little girl stepped out the door and pulled the bell rope. The tinny sound acted like a drain. It emptied the schoolyard, sucking and swirling the children right into the door of the little building. Emily let herself be pulled along through a coatroom full of hooks and shelves that held only the pails of three children who wouldn't be walking home for lunch.

She emerged in a room crowded with neat rows of benches. Every seat had room enough for two children, with a shared tabletop extending from the seat just ahead. Across the front of the room stretched a square of black-painted boards, and in the back corner, close to where she stood, a coal heater squatted beneath a flue that rose through the ceiling.

A man sat writing at a desk on the far side of the room. He was young and capable-looking, unperturbed by the rabble flooding in around him. As Emily watched, he rapped once on the table with a wooden rod, and silence washed over the room like soft rain.

"Good morning, class. We will begin this morning by reciting the Lord's Prayer. Oh, hello," he interrupted himself, catching sight of Emily standing in the back. "You must be Emily Preston. My name is Mr. Marbliss. Your uncle has already registered you."

Moments before, students had pushed past her as if she were a plank on one of the walls. Now every one of them craned their neck to gawk at her. She smirked and shook out her curls.

"What grade are you in, Emily? Your uncle wasn't certain."

She let her words grow slow and broad and Southern. "I don't know. I've never attended school."

"Surely you've had some instruction," he prompted.

She looked down her nose at her new classmates. "Where I come from, we are assigned tutors. We don't cram into a schoolroom like chickens in a coop."

That prompted whispering among the benches. Emily noticed the dark look that passed between two big girls at the back of the room. She smiled sweetly at them.

"Well, you're one of us now," Mr. Marbliss responded shortly. "Take the seat there next to Abby."

Emily marched up to a timid-looking girl and flounced down beside her. The teacher followed with a slate and a few books, which he placed on the desktop.

31

"All right, let's begin," he announced.

The morning passed in a flurry of spelling, grammar, and arithmetic. Emily was assigned to the sixth grade and kept up with her class just fine, except in long division, which she had never been particularly fond of anyway. When Mr. Marbliss dismissed them for recess, the children poured from the desks like sand through an hourglass.

Emily waited for the room to clear before making her way to the grassy schoolyard. Outside, the two girls from the back row stood waiting. One was tall, wispy, and blonde; the other was of medium height, with beautiful dark curls and plump cheeks. Neither looked inviting.

As Emily passed between them, the girls fell into line behind her. She chose to ignore them and settled on a stump at the side of the building. A few girls played hopscotch nearby on a grid they had scratched in the mud. The rest of the children tore around in circles, throwing a ball at each other and shrieking like savages.

Just then the ball flew her way, and before she could duck, it struck her in the shoulder. It didn't hurt, but the laughter of her schoolmates brought sharp color to her cheeks. Angrily, she snatched up the ball and heaved it across the road.

"Did they hurt you?" a voice mocked at her elbow. "Poor dear. Perhaps you could have them stripped and beaten, just like at home." It was the dark-haired girl.

The blonde came up on her other side. "You're a regular princess, aren't you? Maybe we should put our shawls down so you don't get your dainty little bum all dirty." Their laughter held no cheerfulness.

Emily glowered, "What do you want?"

Instead of answering, they crowded onto the stump on either side of her. The blonde continued, fingering the lacy edge of Emily's skirt. "What a beautiful dress. European, no doubt. And satin slippers to match. Too bad they got so dirty. You should have stayed in your castle with your tutor instead of scratching around in the mud with all of us *chickens*."

Emily strode away with a toss of curls, but the girls followed, bolder now.

"It's true, isn't it?" the brunette spoke again. "You are a princess, with a big house and a room full of china dolls and your own pony and," she fixed Emily with a stare, "a village full of slaves."

The accusation was meant to make her squirm, but Emily answered smugly. "Two hundred and thirteen of them. Ella Wood is the fourth largest estate in Charleston County."

The girl held her gaze. "How does it feel wearing fine clothes, driving a fine carriage, living in a fine house, knowing you didn't earn any of it?"

Emily's eyes flashed. "My father is the hardest-working man I know."

"Do you honestly believe it's right for one person to own another?" the girl challenged.

Emily's chin came up, her blue eyes boring into the dark ones. She could almost hear sparks flicking between them. "I do."

As they stood locked together, the blonde sighed in mock dismay. "That's such a pity. My daddy told me about the bad place people like you will go to someday."

Emily tore herself away and smiled sweetly at the girl. "Oh, I know all about that, sugar. My parents sent me there just this week." She flounced toward the door just as the recess bell rang.

Emily spent most of penmanship class watching customers go in and out of the dry goods store across the street. Mr. Marbliss had to reprimand her three times. And she had barely half of her history assignment read before school was dismissed for lunch. At her teacher's insistence, she brought

33

the textbook home.

Her uncle was true to his word. "How'd it go?" he asked when she reached the corner where he waited.

"Splendidly," she groused. "The teacher drives us like mules, and the lovely girls I sit by are spawned from dragons."

"That bad, huh?"

"They think I'm some kind of devil because I come from a slave-holding family."

"And you didn't flaunt that, I'm sure." His voice held sarcasm. "You'll have to get used to that around here. In some circles, sympathies lie pretty heavily with the slave."

He led her through the kitchen's back door where the thick, yeasty smell of fresh bread wafted over them. At the cookstove, the black serving woman was stirring a big pot that sent up heavenly vapors.

"Emily, this is Julia Watson. She runs my kitchen, and I couldn't have chosen a finer cook. Julia, my niece, Emily Preston."

The black woman nodded and offered an even "How do you do?" but her eyes remained aloof.

"She keeps the room at the back of the kitchen, there. Her son bunks with Zeke. He'll be along soon. And you've already met Shannon, I believe. She lives across town with her sister's family."

"Hello, Emily." The red-haired woman smiled at her from a work table where she sliced crusty loaves of bread.

Emily stiffened. "You may continue to call me Miss Preston, please."

Shannon's smiled faltered. "Of course, miss," she stated with an uncertain glance at Isaac.

Her uncle let the moment pass with a slight shake of his head. "I always eat lunch in the kitchen," he informed Emily, drawing a chair up to a simple wooden table in the corner. "I prefer the informality. Come join me."

She slid onto a bench pushed against the wall. Julia brought them each a steaming bowl of vegetable soup and two thick slices of bread. The meal was simple but delicious. While she ate, Emily noticed Shannon slipping in and out of the dining room serving a few guests.

Her uncle told her, "I might not be here when you get home from school. I need to haul a load of firewood from my timber lot west of town, but Shannon will be here. A few guests checked out this morning, and their rooms need cleaning. Shannon will help you get started."

Emily's mouth tightened. Twice more she had wrangled with her uncle on that subject, even pitched a screaming, kicking tantrum in the middle of the lobby, but all to no effect. She was about to launch into further objections when a figure burst through the kitchen door like a runaway team. When it stopped to drop a pile of books on the table, Emily could see it was a colored boy a little taller than herself.

Julia whirled from her place at the stove and threatened the boy with a wooden spoon. "Malachi Watson, you go back out dat door and come in proper, you hear?"

The boy hunched up his shoulders and ducked his head like a sunflower drooping over its stem. "Yes, Mama."

Isaac chuckled. "He's just being a boy, Julia."

"Dat's no boy. He a wild animal." She stirred the soup, talking low and fast. "Ain't no wild animal gonna live under dis roof if I gots sumpin' to say about it, no sir. He can jus' go back outside and act like a son o' mine."

By this time the boy had come back in and was grinning sheepishly at Isaac. The man waved him over.

"Malachi, this is my niece, Emily Preston. Emily, this is Julia's son, Malachi."

"It's fine to meet you," Malachi said with a grin that revealed even white teeth.

Emily looked the boy over. He had skin the color of strong tea before the cream was added, and his eyes were as

35

dark as the midnight sky. They sparkled with intelligence and humor. His black hair was rather long and gave him a couple extra inches in height.

Julia plunked the simple meal in front of her son. "Chil' gots no sense. No sense at all," she muttered.

"You from down south?" he asked.

Emily ignored him but he didn't seem to notice. "I've never been south. Mama and Daddy have been there, but they came north when they were freed. I was born right here in Detroit."

Julia set a glass of milk in front of the boy. "You's one o' de lucky ones."

Emily pulled her history book out and began to read without another glance at either of them, but Malachi was unabashed.

"I have homework too," he stated, patting his own pile of books. "Sometimes it can get pretty heavy. I have to walk all the way from Second Baptist Church. That's why I was late to lunch."

Emily looked up in surprise then snorted down into her pages. A colored school? Everyone knew black people couldn't learn, but in Michigan they had their own school!

Julia cast dark looks at her from the stove, making her own opinions abundantly clear.

First Shannon's disrespect, now Julia's. Emily glanced at her uncle to gauge his reaction, but he seemed completely oblivious. She sniffed in disdain. Isaac didn't seem to have much control in his own house.

Ezekiel came through the dining room door. "Marse Isaac, you's got cus'umers dat wants a room."

"Thank you, Zeke." Her uncle wiped his mouth on a napkin and excused himself.

Ezekiel immediately set to work washing dishes. When they were clean and stacked in their places, he puttered around the kitchen helping Julia with odd jobs.

Emily frowned. Zeke wasn't her uncle's hired labor. He was here to serve her. He was one servant she could control.

"Zeke!"

The dignified old man answered immediately. "Yes, miss?"

"Zeke, my soup is cold," she pouted. "Get me a new bowl."

He bowed. "Sho' thing, miss."

Malachi fell silent, watching, and Julia glared at Emily from across the room as she slopped a ladleful of soup into a new bowl. Zeke delivered it stolidly.

"Dat be all, miss?"

"No. I want another piece of bread. This time with butter on it."

The loyal old slave did exactly as she bid. When he returned, she flicked her silverware off the edge of the table.

"Oh, clumsy me. I've knocked my spoon onto the floor. Zeke, be a dear and pick it up."

Malachi's eyes grew black as he watched the old man struggle to bend over. Emily smiled triumphantly. At least Zeke still knew his place.

Malachi jumped from his chair, scooped up the spoon, and with a pointed look at Emily, handed it to the old man. Emily frowned and swiped it from Zeke's outstretched hand. "Thank you, Zeke," she snapped, glaring at the boy.

Julia leaned up against a work table, her arms crossed in front of her. "If you's done with yo' display, Miss Emily, it's 'bout time fo' yo' school to start."

"I'm not going back," she challenged. "I hate school."

Malachi still stood where the spoon had fallen. "That seems mighty foolish, if you ask me."

"I didn't."

"There's some folks who would pay anything for what you're casting away. If you're having trouble with your studies, I could help you after supper."

Emily laughed out loud. "What could you possibly teach me?"

He met her eyes evenly. "Maybe nothing. Maybe something."

Her uncle popped his head through the outside doorway. He had changed into patched trousers with red suspenders pulled up over a stained and frayed shirt. His unruly hair poured over his forehead. "Ready to go, Emily? You get your wish. The school's on the way to my timber lot outside of town. You may catch a ride on the wagon if you want."

She looked him up and down and almost refused. He looked like a cross between a lumberjack and a character from a minstrel show. But she remembered the muddy streets. With an exaggerated sigh, she slapped her book shut.

Malachi smiled, his manner casual and easy once again. "See you later."

She threw him a withering glare as she followed her uncle from the kitchen.

Outside, the team was hitched to an old buckboard wagon with several tools strewn about the box, along with an old, wadded tarpaulin. Her uncle handed her up to the seat and climbed beside her. She felt like a peasant as they drove out of the yard.

"Where do you hide this contraption?" she asked.

"I own that barn down the road," he answered, pointing. The brick storage building looked like a hundred others in the city. "Why?" he grinned. "Don't you like it?"

"I can't say I've ever had the misfortune to ride in one before. Why on earth don't you hire this done? Or burn coal?"

"Because wood is free, save for a little labor, and I like the work. A fellow can get stir-crazy sitting indoors all day."

38

"Well, drop me off before the school comes into view, please."

He chuckled. "If you insist." Then he turned serious eyes on her. "Emily, I'd like to speak to you about Shannon."

"I'd like to speak about her as well," she interrupted. "It's improper, the way she addresses you. You are the son of a wealthy planter; she's a scullery maid."

A muscle jumped in his jaw. "She's a delightful woman who would like to befriend you."

"I wouldn't be friends with her if she was the last person in Detroit."

His words became low and rough, like they'd been scraped over gravel. "Then she will respect that. But I demand you show her equal respect, because next spring Shannon is going to become your aunt. She has agreed to marry me."

Chapter Five

"We have three rooms to clean tonight," Shannon instructed as she led the way upstairs with a bucket of hot, soapy water. Cheerful as always, she seemed to have forgotten the awkward moment in the kitchen that noon. She turned into the first room at the top of the stairs. "To begin, we make the bed. If you'll get on the other side, miss, we'll do it together."

Emily approached the bed hesitantly. She didn't have the faintest idea what to do.

"All right, grab the blankets and pull them up, like this."

With one tug, Shannon's capable hands had her half of the bed smooth. Emily yanked at the top quilt, only to have the linens underneath bulge and wrinkle. By the time she worked them flat, she had mussed Shannon's side.

"No, no. Just grab them all together and tug, like this. Then take the pillow, fluff it up nice, place it at the top, and fold the quilt up over it, just like that."

Emily looked hopelessly at the neat bedding. She'd never get her side so perfect.

"You work at it," Shannon encouraged, "while I start sweeping."

As the maid waltzed and hummed around the room,

Emily tugged and smoothed, but when one side seemed right, the other would pull crooked. She'd start over, only to find a lump where there hadn't been one before. Her fingers were as clumsy with the bedding as they were with her clothing.

"I'm going on to the next room," Shannon called from the doorway. "When you finish, start mopping the floor."

At last, Emily smoothed out the worst of the bumps. She set the pillow in place, pulled the quilt over it, tucked it in, and stood back to admire her work. But like an uncooperative child, the pillow had created all sorts of new bulges. She finally gave it up in frustration.

Turning to the mop bucket, she stared at it doubtfully. She had seen the house slaves at home on their hands and knees scrubbing away at the floors. It didn't look like something she cared to learn.

She knelt down, careful not to let the hem of her dress touch the floor, and pulled the rag up by one corner. It came with a rush of water. Pinching it with two fingers, she held the streaming cloth at arm's length and dragged it lightly over the floorboards. Dipping it again, she turned and let the stream run on her other side. Soon a sloppy, soapy sea of water surrounded her. She perched on a dry circle like a castaway on a desert island.

By this time, the strong lye soap had begun stinging her hand. She cried out, dropping the rag onto the streaming floor, and popped her burning fingers into her mouth. The soap tasted awful.

Shannon poked her head in the door. "What's the matter?" she asked, then caught sight of the floor with dismay. "Oh dear."

The woman knelt beside the bucket and reached in with both hands. Gripping the rag, she wrung it out tightly and pressed it into Emily's hand. "I'm afraid this is no afternoon tea party, miss. You're going to have to get down on the floor and scrub."

Emily looked at the maid with her rough, work-reddened hands. Her uncle had his choice of any blue-blooded belle in Charleston, and this was the woman he had chosen to become his wife?

"Come on now, on your knees."

"But I'll get my dress all dirty," Emily protested.

"That's no sensible outfit, that's for sure. But if you insist on wearing it, it's going to get dirty. Come on now."

Emily huffed and she pouted, but at last Shannon had her pushing the rag back and forth on the wooden planks. "That's it. Start in the corners and work toward the door. I'll tidy up this bed just a bit." With a flick and a tuck, the quilts lay flat.

"When you're finished, I'll mop the other rooms. I believe this is enough for your first day on the job." With a sympathetic smile, the Irish woman left her alone.

Emily stretched and pulled, scouring away at the wood. Beads of sweat dampened her face and her back began to ache. Over and over—push, pull, push, pull. Her arms were screaming, and the skirt of her beautiful dress was a limp, sodden mess.

As her discomfort grew, so did her temper. And her uncle became the prime target. What right did he have to treat her this way? She was no servant. She hadn't traveled a thousand miles to slave in his hotel.

Her rage worked itself into such a thunderhead that she stormed from the room. If Uncle Isaac wanted the room clean, he could do it himself!

She met Malachi coming up the stairs. He smiled. "There you are. Mama sent me to find—"

Emily slapped the dripping rag into his chest, not caring a crumb for his mama's wishes. She stomped down the stairs, wrathful as a lumberjack fresh out of whiskey. Plowing through the lobby, she glared at a bewildered guest and slammed the door to her room.

Did her mother know this would be expected of her? Emily glanced around for pen and ink and was satisfied to find both in the small writing desk in the corner. She wasted no time.

Dearest Mother,

I have arrived safely, though I cannot assure you I am sound. The journey was frightfully taxing, and now my uncle intends to work me like a common maid. Why, this evening he has me making up bedding and scrubbing the floors. Me! Your daughter! On hands and knees, cleaning a Yankee hotel!

I expect you are as shocked about this as I am, and I trust you'll make arrangements for my homecoming, as I can't bear the indignity your brother has bestowed on me.

I see now why you so seldom mentioned him. He is boorish and rude, and his mockery is completely intolerable. He is also sloppy in his appearance, though at the moment I can say little more for myself. I do wish you had let me bring Lizzie. I simply cannot function without her.

Emily's anger began to wear off, replaced by an empty, sick hollowness. She rested her chin on her fist and gazed out the open window, her thoughts far away. She longed for Ella Wood so much her stomach ached with it.

A soft breeze wafted in around her, lightly perfumed with autumn blooms. What was happening at home? What tasks had Lizzie been reassigned to? Was anyone exercising Chantilly? Had Sophia driven off her latest tutor yet?

Emily missed her good friend and longed to talk with her. Sophia was a few years older than she was, and lately she thought of little else but the next round of parties. Emily hated the idea of being paraded through society in search of a husband, and her friend's enthusiasm could grow tiresome. But Sophia had seen more of the world and could

43

give very good advice. Emily was sure she'd know what to do now.

A movement outdoors caught her attention. The two bloodhounds came trotting into the yard. Their tongues lolled and their fur was completely covered with mud, as if they'd fashioned suits of the stuff to wear about town. They headed directly for the horse trough outside the barn door, planted their forefeet over the rim, and plunged in their muzzles.

Mr. Burrows and his two companions soon followed them into the yard. The men carried shotguns and looked as mud-spattered as their dogs.

"We might as well give it up and go home, fellas," Mr. Burrows was saying. "We've been up and down that river a thousand times. Our boy is gone."

"It's the third trail we've lost this year, boss. And it always disappears right here. Wayne County," Satterfield spat out, "nigra-lovin' capital of the nation. Folks in these parts don't care a whit for the law. Helpin' runaways is stealin' a man's property just as sure as if they raided a slave cabin."

"And they're costing me a fortune." Mr. Burrows' mouth was a hard, thin line. He little resembled the cultured gentleman Emily had bantered with at dinner last night. "If I find out who's behind it…"

With a violent jerk, he slapped the barrel of the gun into his palm.

Chapter Six

Emily pitched the dishwater into the grass outside the kitchen door. She had just finished the last of the supper dishes. Julia remained in the kitchen organizing her work space before retiring for the evening. She could hear the woman inside clanking pans and putting away a few remaining dishes.

Shivering slightly, Emily stepped into the middle of the backyard and looked up at the stars that were beginning to take over the darkening sky. The smell of garbage wafted over the stone wall from the alley beyond, and she could hear the rustle of rats as they fought over the choicest morsels. In the barn a horse whinnied, and the clop of hooves and crunch of wheels sounded on the road beyond the hotel.

Above her she could see Delphinus, the dolphin who had saved the life of the poet, Arion, and been given a place of honor among the constellations by Apollo. And there was the bright *W* that was Cassiopeia, the mortal queen who had dared brag of her beauty to the goddesses. And there the Big Dipper scooped up the Milky Way just as it did back home.

When Emily was a little girl, her father had taken her outside in each season and pointed out the pictures in the stars, explaining the ancient lore behind them. She wondered if he was looking up at the same stars right now.

"They're beautiful, aren't they?"

Emily started. She hadn't heard Malachi approach.

"Looks like you can just reach up and pluck one down, maybe set it in a ring," he said. "It'd be the most beautiful piece of jewelry you ever laid eyes on."

He pointed to the giant dipper. "See the last two stars in the bowl of the spoon? They line up just right and point the way to the North Star."

Emily had learned that when she was six.

"When I was little, I remember Mama setting a candle in the window on the nights Daddy would get in late. I slept sound on those nights, confident that beacon was guiding my daddy home."

He paused as he contemplated the night sky. "The North Star is sort of like a candle that God hung up special to guide His lost children. Lot of black folks looking up at it right now, directing themselves home to freedom."

Emily remained stubbornly silent, like always, even though her rudeness never had any effect on the boy. He went on as if she were holding up her end of a friendly conversation. This time she cut him short.

She hung the washtub in its place and dragged herself inside and to her room. She felt more tired than she ever remembered feeling in her life. Five long days of school and as many evenings of labor had turned her muscles to lead. Well, perhaps not. Lead couldn't possibly hurt so much. But tomorrow was Saturday, and she would demand some rest and some solitude.

A light burned beneath the door to her uncle's office. She entered without knocking and nearly tripped over a pile of garden tools that lay sprawled across the doorway. She stepped over them and approached the desk determinedly.

Isaac hastily slipped a book into a drawer and turned to her with a smile. "Emily, you look exhausted. But I'm

46

proud of you. You've been working hard, and I believe you have earned a day off. What do you say?"

She stalled like a wagon stuck in mud.

"I was thinking you might enjoy some time in Cass Park. You're used to open fields. You must be feeling a bit confined by all these buildings. I've asked Zeke to accompany you for a few hours in the morning.

"It's not Ella Wood, of course, but I believe you'll find the bit of green grass and shade trees quite pleasant. I'll have the carriage ready after breakfast." He paused then and frowned, taking note of her silence. "Unless you have objections…"

She shook her head dumbly.

"Good, then it's all arranged. Sleep well, and I'll see you in the morning."

***

The park wasn't large, only a city block; smaller than her front yard at home. But the grass was soft and the shade inviting. And when she sat down on a blanket with Sophia's penny novel open on her lap, not one building was leaning over her shoulder.

Zeke stayed with the carriage, dozing on the padded seat and soaking the sunshine into his bones. For the first time since leaving home, Emily felt relaxed and free.

She reached into her satchel and pulled out the bread and cheese Julia had packed for her lunch. She nibbled on it as she let the book carry her away to the adventure and romance of the recent Mexican War. It was far more exciting than the usual textbooks provided for her, and she could only imagine her mother's reaction if she ever found out. But eventually Santa Anna was defeated, Mexico ceded over the southwest territories, and the dashing American soldier took the *señorita* home to become his bride. Emily

47

tossed the book aside.

The sun had pushed the shadow of the tree off her blanket, and the fabric of her dress was clinging to the moisture on her back. As she moved to the shade she glanced toward the carriage. Zeke's head had fallen across the back of the seat, and she could see his mouth hanging open. She stifled a giggle. He'd be mortified if he knew he'd been seen in such a position, but it was an opportunity she couldn't pass up.

Pulling her watercolor paper from her bag, Emily penciled in the horses and carriage and detailed the old black man asleep in the seat. Then she took out her paints and breathed life into the scene. Washing in the brilliant blue sky and the living green of the new grass, Emily forgot for a moment that she wasn't home in Ella Wood. The arrogant facade she had adopted on entering the city slid away, and she became fully absorbed in the familiar pleasure of her craft.

Finishing, she scrutinized the painting with satisfaction. She had managed to capture both the tranquility of the morning and the humble demeanor of the sleeping slave. She set the paper in the sun to dry then dug her math book out of her bag. Her fun was over; several long division problems waited to be solved. Mr. Marbliss never sent her away lacking for homework.

That week, she had learned the names of the two girls at the back of the schoolroom. The dark-haired one was Helen Brownstone. Her father had made some money in land investments. He was now active in the new Republican Party and an avid abolitionist. Helen inherited a full share of his fervor and never lost an opportunity to criticize Emily. She was unfailingly joined by Angelina Davis, whose father pastored a local church.

Emily had finished eleven of the math problems and was growing extremely frustrated when Malachi tramped

48

across the park and flopped on the grass beside her. He peered curiously at the painting lying in the grass. "Did you paint that?" he asked.

Emily quickly tucked the damp picture beneath her schoolwork.

He shrugged. "What are you working on?"

Emily frowned. "What are you doing here?"

"Your uncle needed the carriage to meet some guests coming in on the afternoon train. He sent me to fetch Zeke and walk you home when you're ready."

A glance toward the street confirmed that the old man and the carriage were already gone.

Emily resumed her work without another word. As snobbish as she acted toward Malachi, she couldn't figure out why he didn't just give up on her.

The boy turned his head to study her tablet. "You're doing these wrong. You forgot a step here. And here," he said, pointing. "Let me show you."

She jerked the pad away and continued working.

"All right," he leaned back, "but you'll see when you prove them. They won't come out right."

Emily stubbornly finished the nine remaining problems before going back to check her answers with multiplication. She hoped the boy would grow tired and wander off, but he sat patiently beside her and watched her work. And just as he warned, most of her answers did not match. She threw her pencil down in frustration.

"Can I show you now?"

Emily shrugged, not really caring.

He spun the tablet and began reworking the problems, pointing out errors and fixing them. And time and again his answers proved correct.

Malachi handed back the pencil. "Think you can do them now?"

She bit her lip, irritated. Instead of answering, she

shoved the pencil and tablet into her bag, along with the blanket and the math book. "I'm ready to go home now."

Malachi grabbed up the bag and flung it over his shoulder. He was quiet as they walked the few blocks to the inn. Emily peered in a couple store windows, but mostly she just focused on the road in front of her, trying to understand why this colored boy could figure division problems and she couldn't.

Back in her own room, she opened the math text and rechecked the problems, trying to recall the steps Malachi had shown her. But if she had been given a blueprint and been asked to recreate the White House she couldn't have been more mystified.

That evening after dinner, as Julia wiped down her spotless kitchen, Emily spread her history text on the table and pretended to study as she waited for Malachi to appear. When he entered she called him over. "Malachi, can you read?"

He laughed. "Shoot, I sure hope I can. I've been going to school six years now."

She pointed out a random passage in her book. "Read that to me."

He shrugged. "'In 1835, an assassination attempt was made on President Andrew Jackson. A man named Richard Lawrence approached Jackson and aimed two pistols at him. Both misfired. The angry Jackson then attacked Lawrence with his cane until his aides restrained him.

"'Lawrence was apprehended and later told authorities he was King Richard III of England, who had been dead some three hundred and fifty years. Clearly insane, Lawrence was placed in an institution and never punished for his crime.'"

Malachi looked up. "Is that enough, or do you want me to go on?"

"I've always been told that colored people don't have

the ability to learn to read."

"You didn't think I could figure math either," he pointed out. "Mama said black people aren't allowed to read where you come from because white men are afraid the slaves will revolt if they learn too much. And I suspect they're right."

"That's absolutely ridiculous!" Emily burst out. It couldn't possibly be true. Could it? She glanced down at the book. Were blacks purposefully kept ignorant to maintain control over them? Were there others as smart as Malachi?

"Can your mama read?"

"She can now."

"Can your daddy?"

He shook his head. "I taught Mama after school each evening."

Ezekiel entered the kitchen at that moment. "Mr. Whittaker in room eight asked for three of yo' oatmeal cookies, Miss Julia."

The woman smiled and handed him the treats and poured a glass of milk as well.

"Zeke," Emily called out. "Can you read?"

"No, miss."

"Malachi, do you think Zeke could learn to read?"

"Sure he could, if someone taught him."

"Zeke, can any of the slaves at Ella Wood read?"

The old man grew guarded. "Colored folk not 'llowed to learn, miss."

"Would you want to read, if you could learn?"

He shook his head and smiled. "No, no. I's too old for all dat now."

But Malachi argued with him. "Zeke, inside a book, you can travel anywhere you want to go and experience things never open to you before. You could read the great classics. And just think, Zeke, you could read the Bible for yourself, instead of just hearing someone else's interpreta-

51

tion of it."

At that, the old slave's eyes grew softer. "It would be nice to see what de Good Book say 'fore I pass on t' Glory." He went out the door with the snack.

"Malachi, could you teach Ezekiel to read?"

"'Course I could, if he wants to learn."

"Good. Do it," she demanded.

Julia wiped her hands on a towel and crossed her arms disapprovingly. "Miss Emily, why you doin' this? You want dat old man to better hisself, or you just tryin' to prove somethin'?"

Emily didn't answer.

The woman continued. "You know, I tol' Ezekiel he could jus' disappear into the crowds one day. It would be easy fo' him to gain his freedom. They's lots of folk would help him."

Emily stiffened. Would the faithful old servant betray her parents' trust?

"But he gots a powerful love fo' you and yo' family, and I hopes you 'ppreciate it. 'Cause he tol' me he a'ready gots his papers. He a'ready free."

Chapter Seven

The road wasn't as muddy today, but Emily took careful steps to avoid the piles of manure. Over the last week, Malachi began accompanying her to school as far as her turnoff then continued on through the center of town. She didn't mind his company so much anymore. It was better than walking alone. They never said much, just trotted along in silence, but it was comfortable. Different than time spent with Sophia, where every second must be filled up with chatter.

But today she was eager for him to be on his way. Today she was not about to suffer the righteous indignation of Angelina and Helen. Nor was she going to endure the crowded classroom and an endless string of assignments. No, today she had other plans.

She bid farewell to Malachi as usual and waited half a minute before slipping back the way they had come. She knew her uncle was leaving that morning to help a friend fix his roof; he had said as much at breakfast. So she waited in an alley until he led the horses down the street to his storage barn and rode out in that awful wagon. Then she zipped around the hotel—the side opposite the kitchen—and slipped into the stable.

She went immediately to the beautiful black mare and

offered her the carrots she had pinched at breakfast from the pile Julia was peeling. It was one of four horses left in the barn. Her uncle's team was pulling the wagon, but three guests were boarding animals.

The mare, she had learned, was named Coal Dust and belonged to a neighbor. Which one she didn't know or care, though she was pretty sure it was a woman, because last night she had found a lady's saddle in the tack room beyond the stalls.

That discovery had started the cogs in Emily's mind to spinning. She had visited the beautiful mare several times, missing the long rides on Chantilly and longing for the open fields of home. But finding that saddle had moved her out of the realm of dreaming and into the possibility of *acting*. She was up half the night planning.

Emily entered the tack room and pulled out the riding habit she had hidden there. Her mother had tried to talk her out of packing it, claiming she would have no use for it in the city, but Emily had insisted. Now she was glad she did.

She slipped out of her dress, stashed it in the hiding place, and stepped into the lovely habit and a pair of low-heeled boots. She laid a saddle cloth on the mare's back and centered the lady's saddle on top, raising the single stirrup as high as it would go. The horse stood quietly as, with a few expert loops and tugs, Emily tightened the girth strap. Then she slipped the bit into the mare's mouth, grabbed up her gloves and a riding crop, and led the horse to a granite mounting block at the door of the stable.

This was the risky moment. If Julia chose to look out the window now, her fun would be over before it even began.

She climbed smoothly onto the saddle, slipping her left foot into the stirrup and securing her right leg above her left, between the two pommels. Firmly seated, she tugged on the reins, spinning the horse toward the lane. But just as she passed the kitchen door, it opened and a washtub full of dishwater cascaded to the gravel beneath the horse's prancing hooves.

The black woman's eyes widened in surprise, and she called out, "Miss Emily, what—?" but she was too late. With a wild cry and a slap of the crop, Emily urged the mare around the hotel and out to the road.

After a block or two Emily pulled back to a slow trot, guiding the horse through the labyrinth of streets her uncle had taken on the way home from the train depot. When she got to the open market, she turned down Michigan Avenue, recalling that it followed a straight route to the countryside.

Morning traffic was heavy, but after a few blocks it began to lessen. Emily had ridden ponies since she was three years old and had received Chantilly for her tenth birthday. She felt confident and in control, and Coal Dust was behaving like a lady, so at the outskirts of town Emily laid on the crop again.

The mare was eager to run. They flew past the last few streets and were suddenly out of town, the confining prison of buildings receding quickly behind them.

The road was broad and level, and as long as she stayed on it Emily had no fear of becoming lost. The tightly packed neighborhoods gave way to sprawling farms with fields of green and gold, and the trees—how she had missed seeing trees!—were arrayed in their autumn coats of many colors, just like Joseph in the Bible story. Back home the foliage would still be lush and green, with hardly a thought yet for winter.

Fence posts zipped along on both sides of the road. Emily passed a field full of pumpkins turning from pale green to brilliant orange. A little farther on, a herd of black-and-white dairy cows grazed in a sunny meadow, having been turned out to pasture after the morning milking.

After several miles, the distance between farms

stretched longer, with more woodland in between. The road began to narrow and developed deep, muddy ruts. Emily pulled Coal Dust back to a walk.

They clumped over a wooden bridge. Off to her right, a small, wandering stream cut diagonally through a meadow of knee-high grass. Beyond the creek grew a fringe of vibrant foliage. Emily decided it was a perfect spot to dismount and let Coal Dust have a rest and a drink.

Still holding the end of one rein, Emily stretched out in the grass and wondered what her uncle was doing right now. She chuckled softly. She had intended to slip away unnoticed, but perhaps it was best that she had made a stir, since Isaac had been too dense to figure out the dog incident. She'd get sent home yet!

She was just wishing she had packed her paints and a bit of lunch when a shout brought her to her feet. "You, girl! Whot you doin' on my land. Cain't ya read!"

Jumping up, she spotted an old, grizzle-haired man peering at her from behind the bushes across the creek. He wore dirty, fringed buckskins, and his beard was as stained as a spittoon. Something in his hand gleamed silver.

"Civ'lization might be creepin' in all 'round me," he muttered regretfully, "but I'll be durned if I can't keep it off my land!"

Emily regained her composure. "I don't see any notice of private property," she challenged.

"It's there, sweetie, and I'm also tellin' you straight out—you ain't welcome."

She lifted her chin smartly. "And you, sir, are an ill-mannered, indecorous old villain!"

A high-pitched cackle wavered across the meadow grass. "Reckon you nailed me proper there. Now get a move on 'fore I need to make use of Hercules, here," he ordered, and pointing the shotgun into the air, he fired.

The blast crackled across the meadow like shattering

56

glass. Coal Dust screamed and reared, jerking the line from Emily's hand. Before Emily could recover, the horse leaped the stream and streaked down the road in the direction of the city.

Wheeling, Emily shouted at the old man. "Now look what you've done!"

The cackle came again. "Best you start walkin', girlie." And still laughing, the man withdrew into the cover of the trees.

"Oh!" Emily steamed, stamping her foot. Her boot left a deep impression in the soft stream bank. She muttered curses at the despicable old man, but with nothing else for it, she recrossed the bridge and started for town, slapping her crop against her thigh in frustration.

She judged she had traveled seven or eight miles out of the city, and it was hours before she finally caught sight of any buildings stretching skyward in the distance. Stomach rumbling, she filled her pockets from a nearby apple tree and plodded on toward the first outlying neighborhoods.

For an hour she watched her shadow stretch in front of her, long and thin like a fast-growing weed. Now it suddenly disappeared. Glancing behind, she caught sight of a black cloudbank silently chasing her down. She began to run and gained the relative protection of downtown before the drops began spilling all around her, sending up little puffs of dust.

She sheltered in a doorway, panting, and watched the street lick up the moisture then begin to dampen and stream as the storm gathered intensity. She closed her eyes and leaned wearily against the building, her legs shaky and her feet feeling like two gigantic blocks of wood. Her carefully planned outing had turned disastrous. She wondered briefly where Coal Dust had gone off to.

Her ear was suddenly grabbed from behind, and she was dragged unceremoniously from her shelter. "Yo' game be up, Miss Emily. What call you got to frighten Mr. Isaac like you done?"

She recognized the voice of Julia Watson. The woman wrenched her ear so hard she was forced to march up the street through the pelting rain on the tips of her toes. One misstep and the lobe was sure to rip clean off.

"You's a ungrateful chil'," the woman continued. "Gots half de city out lookin' fo' you. Don't you know any better than to go traipsin' off without tellin' a soul where you's goin'?"

They found Isaac astride Barnabas in the middle of Washington Street. His face was hard and expressionless, like a sheet of iron. Emily wished he would just rant and rage at her. This unreadable emotion frightened her.

"She was sittin' in the do'way of a lawyer's office like some wretched little waif."

One eyebrow arched skyward. "Are you planning to sue someone, niece?" he asked coldly.

Oh, she hated his mockery! It fueled her weary muscles and her temper. Her ear released, she planted her booted feet and faced him squarely. "What I do is no concern of yours!"

"It is when your mother entrusts you to my care. Coal Dust came home hours ago. She throw you?"

She lifted her chin proudly. "Of course not! She pulled free after I dismounted." She wouldn't tell him about the gunshot.

"And you've been walking all this time? How far did you ride? Toledo?"

She glared.

"You had no business on that horse. Climb up and I'll take you home."

But Emily's dander was up, and her face burned like a furnace. "So you can work me like a field hand? So I can clean your hotel? 'Yes, Marse Isaac.' 'No, Marse Isaac.' Well, I won't do it. I refuse to go one step with you!"

58

Isaac's face hardened into flint and his voice was low and steady, like the rumble of a locomotive. "Emily, get on the horse."

"I will not!" she screamed and stomped off in another direction.

His movements were as quick and fluid as falling water. One minute she was storming through the mud down the middle of the road. The next minute she found herself lifted onto the horse. She kicked and screamed, sobbed, struck out and whipped her sodden curls, but the unforgiving steel of Uncle Isaac's arm encircled her waist and held her firmly in place.

Emily caught sight of Julia walking beside them, soaked through, with a mixture of annoyance and satisfaction on her face. She quit fighting, but she rode high and stiff and proud, as far away from Isaac as she could manage.

He chuckled humorlessly. "You are so much like I was at your age. And there was nothing I needed more than a stout hickory stick applied to my backside."

She tensed with horror. He wouldn't dare!

"The world owed me everything, and if it didn't work out as I planned, a good fit of rage usually set things right. But that's no preparation for the real world. I suspect your mother knows it too; that's why she sent you to me. And I don't intend to disappoint her."

Emily didn't like the sound of that. She rode the whole way in stubborn silence, her back as stiff and straight as the trunk of a pine.

Isaac deposited her at the kitchen door. "I sent Malachi after your schoolwork. Your lessons are in your room where you are to stay until I decide your punishment."

Emily pushed inside and found Shannon seated at the kitchen table with her head bowed. She looked up and Emily saw concern melt into relief. "Miss Emily, you're home! I've been so worried! Are you all right?"

Emily showered her with scorn. "I'm fine," she snapped. "I'm not a stupid pet dog that can't find its way home."

"Of course you're not." Shannon rose uncertainly. "May I help you out of those wet clothes?"

But Emily jerked away. "Go mother someone else." She stomped to her room.

Dripping and muddy, Emily climbed onto her bed and shoved the school books to the floor. She considered making another break for it, but it felt so good to lie down. Soon the eerie strains of "Moonlight Sonata" came floating down the hall from the lobby, and her last thought before drifting off to sleep was that she'd never make it past her uncle anyway.

Chapter Eight

The odor of fresh manure assaulted Emily's nose like a right hook. She grasped the handle of the pitchfork, scratched a little at a wet pile on the barn floor, and could almost see the vapors rising from it. She was starting to wish her uncle had settled for the hickory stick.

She had changed into her traveling suit, which was fast becoming a ragged work dress, and covered it with one of Julia's aprons. Not wanting to stain her hands, she'd sacrificed her white riding gloves, intending to throw them away afterwards. A hand-me-down pair of Malachi's boots flopped on her feet, completing the ridiculous costume.

"You're never going to finish at that rate," Malachi stated and rolled a wheelbarrow in place beside her. "And no sense walking out back with every forkful. Pick it up in big chunks and dump it in. Like this."

She was more than willing to give up the tool and watch him wield it, but he handed it right back. She whined, "You're so much better at it than I am. I wasn't born for work, and it's not fair of my uncle to make me do it."

The depths of the boy's eyes went black, as when he'd picked up the spoon for Zeke. "Reckon you had it coming. And breeding has nothing to do with it. Anyone can make up their mind to get a job done. But it does take some grit," he added, as though that was a quality she sorely lacked.

Isaac strolled through the doorway and watched Emily's pathetic attempts. "Julia will keep your supper warm for you. You may eat it when you are finished—after I've inspected your work."

Emily's heart sank. The stolen apples were long gone, and her middle echoed like an underground cavern. Her nap hadn't been nearly long enough, either.

Then Isaac waggled a finger at Malachi. "Don't let her hoodwink you into doing it for her. It was her own foolishness that got her into this."

"Yes sir." He followed Isaac out of the darkening barn, turning to call out, "See you in the morning, Emily."

Their comments rankled like woolen underwear. Did they both think so lowly of her? She was perfectly capable of accomplishing anything she wanted—before morning—and she was plenty stubborn enough to prove them wrong. She set into the muck with a vengeance.

The work was backbreaking, and blisters began to form on her hands, even through the kid gloves. But she wiped the sweat away with the back of her sleeve and worked through the pain until the stalls were spotless. Then she sprinkled straw on the floor, just like her uncle had showed her, and even led the horses back into them. Finally, pitching the fork into the haystack, she went in search of Isaac.

Her uncle looked up in surprise as she came stomping through the kitchen door, but Julia pounced on her before she could speak.

"Out! You take dose filthy boots off 'fore you come traipsin' over my clean floor. And ain't dat my apron you's wearin'? Chil', you don't takes my apron without axin' me firs'!"

Isaac's eyes sparkled. "Would you have given it to her?"

She glared at him. "Do mules dance? Kitchen aprons

ain't fo' cleanin' barns!"

Emily smiled sweetly and handed it to the woman. "You can have it back."

Isaac laughed out loud. Then he rose from the table. "You did that mighty quick, young lady. Let me go see if the job was more successful than your first mopped floor."

Emily sank onto the bench and pushed sweaty hair out of her eyes. Too late, she remembered the gloves. She could feel wetness smeared against her cheek.

Her uncle returned a few minutes later. Malachi came in behind him holding an empty burlap sack which he hung on a nail behind the door.

"Nicely done, my dear. Julia, please fetch this child some supper."

The woman clanked the pans together loudly. "She need a good kick in de pants, dat's what. Skippin' school and frolickin' about de countryside," she muttered, shaking her head.

But Malachi sent her a simple nod that communicated a new respect. It warmed her all the way to her stockinged toes and thawed out some of her pride. But to make it understood that she hadn't melted completely, she lifted her chin and threw him a you-shouldn't't-have-doubted-me look.

Julia plunked down a steaming plate piled with fried chicken, mashed potatoes, and coleslaw. Emily dove in ravenously, setting aside proper etiquette for the moment, as it didn't coordinate with dung-splattered clothing anyway.

When clean bones sat alone on the plate, her uncle dropped an envelope in front of her. "I picked this up today. You'll be happy to know your family hasn't completely forgotten you."

With a little squeal, she scooped up the letter and rushed from the room. Out on the front porch the storm had moved on, and the sleepy sun was pulling a colorful blanket around its shoulders. Emily perched on the railing and caught its parting rays on her mother's handwriting.

Dearest daughter,

I hope this letter finds you fully recovered from your trip and doing well. We miss you too, but your father and I think it is best that you remain with my brother for a while longer. He's a good man and may yet succeed in areas we have failed you. Keep a stiff upper lip and try to make the most of your visit…

She set the letter in her lap and looked out over the skyline of the city. She would not be going home to her beautiful Ella Wood as she had hoped. She was stuck in Michigan indefinitely with a man as unmovable as Lake Huron. She was disappointed, but not as devastated as she thought she might be.

She finished her letter, devouring news of Sophia and her latest antics. Lizzie was well, as was the rest of the household. Her father had bought a new field hand that was causing some problems. He had also purchased a filly that her mother was certain Emily would just adore. Aunt Margaret had come for a visit and sent her love.

Emily tucked the communication back into its envelope. The evening chill was beginning to penetrate her sweat-dampened body, and a hot bath sounded heavenly. Perhaps she could persuade her uncle to fill the tin washtub for her even though it wasn't Saturday.

But she couldn't find him anywhere.

"Yo' uncle had an errand to run tonight. You kep' him busy half de day with yo' shenanigans. When do you 'spects him to get his work done?" Julia asked.

There was always Zeke, she figured. Julia was simply pushing hot air around with all that talk of him being free. But soon after she climbed into her muddy nest of a bed to wait for the old slave to answer her call, she didn't care much about anything.

64

Emily awoke feeling rested, albeit a bit sore, but she soon learned her riding incident wasn't behind her quite yet. Still dressed from the evening before, she swung her feet over the bed where they met the floor with a shocking chill. She hustled to the kitchen, stumbling through the predawn darkness to the promise of warmth and to try again for a bath.

"That's an excellent idea," her uncle agreed. "Malachi, would you set some water on the stove to heat? Emily should look presentable when she meets Mr. Thatcher."

Malachi cast her a sympathetic look before fetching the tin bucket to the pump in the backyard.

"Who's Mr. Thatcher?" she asked.

"William Thatcher and his daughter, Melody, live in that beautiful Victorian home up the road. Mr. Thatcher owns a textile mill by the river. He also owns Coal Dust," he said pointedly.

Emily looked up in alarm. "He doesn't know I took her, does he?"

"No—"

Emily breathed a sigh of relief.

"—which is why we are paying him a visit this morning. You are going to tell him what you did. And apologize."

Her face whitened. "I will not! The horse is home. She's not even hurt!"

"I'm sorry, Emily, but you need to learn to take responsibility for your actions. We'll go before school."

Julia looked on with complete satisfaction. "And after school, you gonna wash dose nasty sheets on yo' bed."

Emily groaned.

The Thatcher house was large and highly ornamented, with steep gables and pointy turrets. Every eave, every angle, every window and door was decorated with carved moldings of various designs and painted in pastel colors. Porches and walkways were railed with black wrought iron, and the overall effect was of bright, airy lightness; a house made of lace.

Emily moved up the concrete walk with no small measure of trepidation, her uncle pushing close behind to ensure she went through with her task. Her knock was answered by a pleasant, round-faced maid who greeted them with enthusiasm. "Why, Mr. Milford, what a pleasure! Come in!"

She ushered them into a parlor off the main hall. "Mr. Thatcher is still at breakfast. He must have his coffee, you know," she smiled. "I'll send him right in."

Isaac remained standing, but Emily sat down on one of the floral sofas, trying her best to shrink into the cushions.

At that moment, a beautiful young woman floated down the stairs in the foyer. She was about twenty years old, slender, with thick dark hair that swooped up under a dainty hat and cascaded in ringlets down her back. She had a parasol tucked under one arm and was just pulling on a pair of gloves when she spotted Isaac.

"Why, Mr. Milford!" she beamed, rushing to his side and clutching his arm. "How lovely of you to come calling! How did you know I just returned from visiting my grandmother? You're the very first gentleman to welcome me home."

Isaac bowed low, "It is my honor, Miss Thatcher."

She swatted playfully at his arm. "Oh, you're such a charmer. But I'm afraid I have a prior invitation that I positively cannot break."

Isaac assumed an expression of deep regret. Miss Thatcher disentangled her arm with a peal of laughter. "Mr. Milford, you keep yourself entirely too preoccupied, tucked away in your little hotel. You simply must come visit me again."

"I'm afraid my business does keep me quite busy," he admitted.

"No excuses," she admonished, moving toward the door. "If you don't call soon enough to suit me, I may show up at your hotel for dinner."

Isaac followed her into the entryway and opened the door for her. "I will save you the seat of honor," he stated with another bow.

She giggled as she stepped outside. "I won't forget now!"

"She's pretty," Emily prompted when the girl was gone. "And wealthy."

Isaac nodded. "And silly. And spoiled."

"Milford!" a voice boomed out before Emily could reply. A stomach showed at the doorway ahead of the rest of the man. When he appeared in full, Mr. Thatcher looked more like a swollen rain barrel than a man, and all the hair from the top of his head had gravitated to the bushy mustache above his lip. "You son of a rascal! What brings you here? That mare of my daughter's giving you trouble?"

"Hello, William. Actually that is why we're here. Emily?"

Mr. Thatcher raised his eyes and glanced around the room, finally spotting the girl. "I say, Milford! I didn't know you had a cub."

Isaac waved her over and Emily reluctantly complied. "This is my niece, Emily Preston. Emily, Mr. William Thatcher."

"How do you do?" Emily mumbled, dropping a small curtsy.

"Well, well," Thatcher muttered, looking her up and down. "Bit runty, ain't she?"

Emily fixed him with a steely glare. Isaac did his best to swallow his amusement. "Er, we're working on that. Emily does have something to tell you, though." And he pushed her to the front.

Emily coldly took note of Mr. Thatcher's fine velvet waistcoat, the watch chain that spanned it, and a fine pair of soft leather boots. He was as unsophisticated as a backwoods farmer, but he obviously had money.

"I ain't got all day, missy," he grumbled.

She lifted her chin. "I admire your riding mare very much, Mr. Thatcher. She's a fine animal. High-spirited and intelligent. But I noticed she's tending toward corpulence. A family trait, I see," she added with a glance at his middle.

"Wha's that?" Thatcher asked, looking to Isaac.

Her uncle shot Emily a stern look. "She says your horse is getting fat."

"Ah, well, Melody doesn't get out to ride her like she should."

"Which is why I took the liberty of exercising her for you yesterday," Emily finished.

His eyebrows shot upward and he glanced from Isaac to Emily. "Then, I suppose I should thank you for it."

Emily smirked triumphantly at her uncle.

"But," Isaac interposed, "she should have asked your permission first, and she should have gone after school hours, and she should have notified someone as to where she was going." He was looking hard at Emily. "She seems to have forgotten this is not her father's plantation. And she has come to apologize."

Emily clenched her jaw. "I'm sorry, Mr. Thatcher."

But the man seemed not to hear. "She your Southern kin?"

"Yes, my sister's daughter from Carolina."

68

"They grow cotton?"

"Some. Rice, primarily."

He nodded, forgetting about Emily altogether. "I want to contact them. Been having trouble with a supplier and I need some new sources to keep running at capacity."

"I'm sure that can be arranged," Isaac said. "In the meantime, Emily would like to make her mistake up to you."

Emily froze. Thatcher looked at her as though seeing her for the first time. "Well," he considered, "she could work a few shifts in the mill."

Emily cut her eyes over to her uncle. He had to be joking!

Isaac pretended to consider the suggestion. "Perhaps it would be wiser to make the punishment fit the crime. What if she took over the care of your daughter's mare? She could feed and water it, keep the stall clean, and with your permission, make sure the horse received regular exercise."

Emily caught her breath as Thatcher scratched at his bushy mustache. She hardly dared believe what she was hearing!

"Well," Thatcher mused, "Melody is often gone visiting. Perhaps that would work out just fine."

Isaac moved toward the door. "Very well. Then if we're agreed, Emily needs to be getting on to school. Thank you, William."

The big man grasped the doorknob in his meaty hand and let his guests out. "Good day, Milford," he boomed. "And if you ever need to let the girl out to work, the offer at my mill stands."

***

A few days later, after a quiet Sunday supper in the kitchen, Isaac leaned back with a satisfied stretch. Julia and

Shannon had finished serving guests and had taken their own supper at the table with Isaac and Malachi and Emily. Zeke puttered with the dishes. He would not eat until Isaac had finished no matter how the younger man tried to persuade him to join them.

"I do love this season of the year," Isaac said, reaching for a small volume on the table beside him. "It puts me in mind of Longfellow."

Emily watched him riffle through the pages. He was often in mind of the poet—his favorite, she had learned—and was in the habit of quoting him at odd times, or of reading aloud, as he did now.

"...*Within the solemn woods of ash deep-crimsoned,*
And silver beech, and maple yellow-leaved
Where Autumn, like a faint old man, sits down
By the wayside a-weary. Through the trees..."

"Why doesn't he just say what he means," Emily interrupted with some impatience, "that he wants to walk through the woods in the fall. It'd be simpler."

Isaac met her eyes. "Where's the music in that?"

She dismissed the question with a shake of her head. "You have to dig through all those extra words. Nobody really talks like that. Novels, on the other hand, are easy to understand because they say just what they mean."

The women politely continued their meal, but Malachi's eyes followed each speaker.

"The beauty of poetry is in the cadence and in the rhyme," Isaac countered.

"It's forcing words to follow rules."

"Ah, rules." Isaac exchanged an amused glance with Malachi. "Don't novelists also conform to some guidelines when they craft their words into a story?"

But Emily backed her opinion firmly. "With poetry,

you have to twist and manipulate the words to make them fit exactly. It's unnatural."

Isaac pursed his lips thoughtfully. "Perhaps achieving beauty inside boundaries is what makes poetry an art."

He closed the book and set it on the table, changing the subject with a simple announcement. "The state fair opens this Tuesday. Shannon and I will be going, and we wondered if Emily and Malachi would like to take a day off school and join us?"

Malachi's wide grin was all the answer he needed to give.

The suggestion awoke Emily's indomitable curiosity, but she answered coolly, "I suppose it's better than a day with Marbliss."

"*Mr.* Marbliss," her uncle corrected. "We'll leave after breakfast."

Chapter Nine

Tuesday dawned warm and breezy. After feasting on Julia's ham and eggs and hashed potatoes, Isaac hitched up the team to the open carriage and they drove out of town to a farm on the east side of the city where an eighty-acre field served as provisional fairgrounds. On one side, booths were set up in rows and plastered with broadsides that advertised everything from yard goods to livestock remedies. The meadow beyond had been flattened by two dozen large agricultural machines that now slumbered in ragged rows. And farther still, a series of temporary shelters and corrals housed all manner of farm animals.

Horses and buggies were parked along the perimeter fence and spilled into the open field adjacent to the festivities. Isaac drove past them and set the brake in an unoccupied corner. Then he helped Shannon down from the carriage. "Need a hand?" he asked Emily, but she had already scampered out after Malachi.

After tethering the team on short leads, Isaac led the foursome to the gate where he paid each twenty-five cent admission.

"You two stick together now, you hear?" he told the children. "I don't want to lose either of you in the crowd."

Malachi stopped to answer, "Yes sir," but Emily was

too busy gawking at the sights. She didn't even bother to pretend indifference.

The very first booth held a variety of new kitchen gadgets which Shannon stopped to admire. "Wouldn't Julia just love to see these?" she commented, spinning an odd-shaped spoon.

Emily couldn't work out any use for the strange utensil, nor did she care. She craned her neck to see the daguerreotypes displayed in the next booth. They were mostly images of families and stern-faced individuals looking head-on at the camera. A fellow from a local studio was sitting behind the table taking appointments.

The next booth advertised the Ladies Missionary Society of the First Methodist Church and announced their afternoon bake sale. Emily's neck swiveled from one sight to the next. She could hardly take in all the movement and color and sound. Malachi, she noticed, was keeping up right behind her.

Isaac laughed at their wide eyes. "Entertaining, isn't it? It's been a popular way for farmers to keep up with the latest technology. That's why the fair has made it to its tenth year. And there's always plenty to entertain the ladies. Look there."

Nearby, a handful of women crowded around a booth. At their center sat a woman who was demonstrating a curious black machine. She started a wheel spinning with her hand and kept it going by pumping a pedal with her foot. As she worked, she fed a length of fabric under an iron arm from which a needle zipped in and out.

"A sewing machine!" Shannon exclaimed. "I've heard of them. Look how fast it works! Why, I could sew a whole dress in an evening with one of those."

The other women looked equally impressed, though the seventy-five dollar price tag seemed to dampen some of their enthusiasm.

Emily moved on to the next booth where several kinds of pies were on display. She recognized rhubarb and blueberry, cherry, apple and peach, and there were others she couldn't name. A menu tacked to the counter also advertised meats and breads, cheese, soup, cookies, cakes, pastries and even root beer. Emily's mouth watered though her belly still felt stretched from breakfast.

"What's that?" Malachi asked, pointing to a curious contraption across the aisle. It looked like a barrel filled with soapy water. A man in a black suit and top hat dropped in several items of clothing and turned a crank, sloshing them around.

"Why, it's some kind of machine to wash clothing!" Shannon exclaimed. She watched, fascinated. "Who ever heard of such a thing?"

The man pulled the clothes out with a long stick and plunged them into a barrel of rinse water. Then he threaded a garment through a pair of rollers that squeezed out all the water. When at last he held up a wrinkled shirt, Shannon shook her head. "It seems like a lot of extra work, and it can't possibly get clothes as clean as the old way. I'm afraid that device will never catch on."

Isaac led them through booths containing information on crop rotation, soil preparation, and several new varieties of seed. They stopped once to watch a juggler move through the crowd and then scanned more food booths and admired the ribbon winners for needlework and quilting, and for canned and fresh produce. Finally, after gawking at McCormick's newest combine and watching a demonstration of a massive threshing machine powered by two horses on a treadmill, all four of them were ready for lunch.

They chose a food booth and settled at a table with their meal. Before plunging in, Emily savored the delicious smells of warm bread, spicy meat, and fresh apple cider.

"Are you two enjoying the fair?" Isaac asked, taking a

huge bite of his sandwich.

Suddenly reserved, Emily let Malachi answer for both of them. "Very much, Mr. Milford. Thank you for bringing us."

Just then a young man strolled up the aisle calling out an announcement that he repeated every twenty yards. "Men and women, boys and girls, don't miss the flying show. In fifteen minutes, the daring Tom Landless will demonstrate a remarkable glider, the invention that has brought wings to mankind. The show will take place on the northeast side of the field. Folks of all ages, don't miss this flying show—"

Emily forgot her coldness. She and Malachi pounced on Isaac as eager as two pups about to dive into a plate of roast beef. "May we go, Uncle Isaac? May we?" Emily begged.

"Weeelllll," he drawled, "I was going to have you help me check out those new buggies lined up so pretty across the way and tell me what you think."

Emily blew out her breath impatiently. "I think every one of them is a whole sight better than that horrid wagon of yours."

Isaac laughed out loud. "Here's a dime for each of you. Now go on before you miss the show."

Shoving the last bits of food into their mouths, the children jumped up from the table and followed the crowd. They fell in behind a heavyset woman who plowed through the mass like Moses parting the Red Sea. As they walked, Malachi asked, "Why are you so aloof with your uncle? He's doing his best by you, but you act like a general kicking around some lowly private."

"I don't either!" she exclaimed, her face flushing.

"You do so. You treat everyone that way."

She was furious. "Back home, you'd never be allowed to talk to me like this!"

75

"Well, somebody had to tell you," he retorted. "Besides, you're doing it again!"

As they approached a weathered barn in the corner of the field, Malachi changed the subject. "Do you think this fellow can really fly?"

"Would they advertise a flying show if he can't?" she snapped.

"I reckon not, but I can hardly believe it. Imagine, someone soaring like a bird!"

The barn stood three stories high, with a platform and a block and tackle erected on top. The structure was braced by two cables that stretched far into the field and anchored into the ground with thick posts. In addition, a wide boardwalk extended the whole length of the roof, enclosed with low rails. The crowd stood below pointing and whispering, a mist of excitement rising from them.

A bearded man rode out of the barn on a powerful horse and drove the crowd back. "Stand aside please. We don't want anyone getting hurt. You'll be able to see better from behind the chalk lines."

As he spoke, four more men rolled a curious contraption out the barn door. It consisted of a narrow cart attached to a large canvas sail that had been stretched taut and fastened horizontally overhead. The glider sat on three small wheels, and a fabric tail on a pole jutted from the back like a rudder on a ship.

"The flying machine!" someone called out. "The flying machine!"

The words buzzed through the crowd like a bee through clover, and the bearded man had to herd them behind the chalk line again.

The men attached the vehicle to the block and tackle and slowly raised it to the platform where two more workers maneuvered it into place. Then another figure appeared on the roof. He was dressed in a blazing red jacket and a matching hat that fastened beneath his chin.

The young announcer stepped out of the crowd. "Ladies and gentlemen, let me introduce to you the incredible Flying Tom Landless. He will demonstrate this wondrous glider you see before you. It is an exact replica of the aircraft invented by the late physicist, Sir George Cayley, in Scarborough, England only five short years ago."

The red-clad man lifted a hand to the cheering crowd and casually stepped into the glider. A long rope was attached to a ring at the point of his cart, and its other end was tossed down to the rider who fastened it to his horse's harness.

"Today you are going to see a fantastical demonstration of skill and daring, and of the remarkable genius that has allowed man to soar on wings through the air like the great birds of prey. Mr. Landless, are you ready?"

At his thumbs up, the craft was unfastened from the block and tackle. The fellow on horseback spurred his animal with a whoop and the aircraft lurched into motion. Guided by the rails, it accelerated smoothly down the boardwalk while the crowd below held its breath.

"Ladies and gentlemen," the announcer shouted with a flourish, "I give you Flying Tom and his incredible flying machine!"

A gasp rose from the crowd as the glider rolled off the end of the roof and hung suspended in midair, floating along behind the galloping horse like a giant kite. Then Flying Tom cut the rope, and the magnificent craft glided forward smoothly and gently, steadied by small movements of its tail.

Emily couldn't take her eyes off the amazing sight. She never would have guessed a person could strap on wings and fly, up there with the wind blowing past and the grass streaming below. She longed for such freedom, for such an extraordinary act of defiance. Just like Mr. Landless, she wished she could break through her own restrictions, the ones that seemed most impossible to challenge.

As the glider soared farther away, the crowd began to run after it. Little boys called to each other and tore across the field with their fathers close behind. Women hiked up their skirts and held their hats in place, doing their best to follow and tugging children along behind them. The whole field was a mass of rippling, shouting amazement.

"Come on!" Malachi yelled and took off running. Emily matched him stride for stride, pleased with the look of surprise on his face. She had grown up playing with the slave children and had run a hundred races with them through the back pasture. Now, with the glider hovering closer to the ground, she sprinted faster. She wanted to see it land.

It floated lower and lower, and just as she thought it would slam into the dirt, the man dipped the steering pole and the nose lifted enough for the wheels to bump down hard one time, slowing the craft before the sail toppled over the front and the nose stuck in the earth like a javelin. The crowd erupted in cheers as Flying Tom climbed out of the glider unharmed.

Emily clapped as enthusiastically as the rest. Sophia would never believe her when she wrote home about this!

After enjoying a few moments of triumph, Flying Tom leaped onto the back of the tow horse, and the team of men jogged across the field to roll the glider back to the barn. Slowly, the crowd began drifting away. The show was over.

Emily scanned the rest of the fairgrounds, uncertain how to follow up such a grand display. Malachi stood with his hands in his pockets and kicked a clump of turf. "Want to go see the animals?"

She wrinkled her nose. By comparison, livestock seemed downright dull. "Let's go spend our money. I want something sweet to eat."

There were so many food booths, the fairgrounds were awash in tempting smells. They inspected tables selling candy apples, roasted meats, pastries, cakes and taffy before settling on doughnuts fried in deep fat and coated with sugar icing.

Pastries in hand, they wandered over to a bench set alongside a crude track where six or seven horses were racing, pulling lightweight, two-wheeled carts. Mud flew from their hooves as they jogged past.

Emily took her first bite, closing her eyes in sheer delight. "Mmmm."

Malachi's was already half gone. "Look!" he called with his mouth full. "There's Mr. Lambert and Mr. deBaptiste." He waved furiously at two colored men walking across the field. One of them saw him and nudged the other. Both returned the wave before being swallowed by the crowd.

"They go to my church," the boy explained. "Mr. Lambert is a tailor, and Mr. deBaptiste has done a little bit of everything, I think. He even used to work for President Harrison. He owns a steamship, but some ridiculous law won't let him operate it because he's black, so he had to hire a white pilot."

Malachi always spoke with unwavering confidence in his people, as if they could do anything whites could do. She didn't want to argue with him, so she asked suddenly, "Malachi, where's your father?"

"He's dead."

"What happened?"

"Cholera epidemic, about seven years ago. We had a small farm near Monroe, but Mama and I couldn't manage it alone. Mama sold out and found the position with your uncle. He's a good man, treats us fair."

"How did your parents become free?"

"Daddy was set free when his master died. Then he

worked six years to buy Mama. She had a brother who escaped a few years earlier. Before leaving, he told her he was heading to Detroit, and if she ever got away to look for him there. So Mama and Daddy came here but never found him. We don't even know if he's still alive."

Emily frowned, unmoved. Malachi's uncle was a runaway who had broken all sorts of laws and cost his owner a lot of time, money and energy. She replied, rather sharply, "You're free, your mama has a job, and you go to school. I should think you'd be satisfied with that."

Malachi gazed at her for a long moment. When she met his eyes she found pity there, along with wisdom and sorrow that made him seem years older. She squirmed, suddenly uncomfortable.

"That may be all some folks are willing to give me," he said softly, "but that isn't all I plan to take. Not by a mile. Emily, someday I'm going to be a doctor."

Emily's eyes grew round. "You're crazy!"

"No, I'm not. White physicians won't treat Coloreds, unless you count the ten-cent quacks who prescribe whiskey and sheep dung. I want to learn how diseases work and what stops them. I want to help my people.

"There's a doctor at my church, a black man with the training he's been able to find for himself. He says there's a new medical school in Ann Arbor, not far away. It's the best in the nation."

"They won't let you in."

"Maybe not, but I can read their books. I want to learn. I can begin to change the way things are."

Emily shook her head in disbelief. Malachi Watson had the most fantastic ideas she ever heard. If he was a slave at Ella Wood, she was sure he'd give her daddy no end of trouble.

He turned the tables on her. "What are you going to do when you get older?"

She snorted. It wasn't as if girls had many choices. "I know what I won't do. I won't let my parents force me into some marriage just because the man is rich."

Malachi stared at her. "Would they do that?"

Emily rolled her eyes. "It's the way things are done in the South. Once a girl gets old enough, she's flaunted before every bachelor in the county to secure a future for her."

He tipped his head curiously. "And you don't want to get married?"

"It's not that I wouldn't marry; I just don't want to be forced into it. I hate everyone telling me it's expected of me. I feel like one of the plants in Uncle Isaac's garden, forced to grow in a box without any freedom."

"And if you had that freedom, what would you choose?"

She had never told anyone her dream before. Not even Sophia. She hesitated, then remembered the glider defying gravity, astonishing everyone. She lifted her chin. "I want to paint."

"Why can't you do that when you're married?"

She shook her head. "No, I mean I want to go to school and study painting. I want to learn how to capture the beauty of a horse in motion, to recreate the sunset over the fields. I want to sell my work and earn my own wages."

"Then, Emily Preston, I think you should do it." He said it like that settled the matter.

Malachi stood and held out a hand to help her up. "Come on. Let's go see the animals."

Emily stared at the dark skin that looked so unlike her own. The two of them were different: black and white; poor and wealthy; the son of slaves, the daughter of privileged landowners. Very different. Too different.

She stood without help.

Chapter Ten

"—then he pounded nails through the barrel, put his offending slave inside, and rolled him down the hill."

Emily sat on the steps of the schoolhouse listening to Helen and Angelina whispering just within hearing distance, baiting her, but she refused to be taken in.

She fingered the lacy edge of her fine damask skirt and watched the younger children at their games. After a few weeks of working in her lovely dresses and watching the beautiful fabrics wear out, she had finally accepted two simple cotton calicoes and a pair of sturdy leather button-up shoes. But she absolutely refused to wear them to school.

Angelina stepped closer. "Tell me, Princess, how do you punish your people?"

Emily sighed. The girls were always questioning her about the most awful things. Emily couldn't convince them that she had never, ever seen such atrocities on her father's plantation. Oh, she had heard vague rumors of cruel overseers now and then, but her father was a gentleman.

"Have you ever bought a slave from Africa?" Helen asked.

"That's been illegal for decades."

"That doesn't mean it doesn't happen. My father says when a boat arrives everyone just looks the other way. So have you?"

Emily shook her head. "Daddy only buys American-born slaves. He says the others are too much trouble."

"Can you blame them?" Helen asked. "If it was me, I'd try to escape. Runaways come through here all the time."

Emily looked at her shrewdly. "Bet you've never even seen one."

Helen fixed her with a challenging stare. "My father gives them food and clothing and helps them get across the river to Canada."

"Then," Emily declared smugly, "your father is a hypocrite. He's breaking the law just as surely as the slavers."

"It's not the same at all."

"Of course it is. Haven't you ever heard of the Fugitive Slave Law?"

The girl shrugged and Emily knew she had, but she reminded her just the same. "It was written eight years ago, and it says anyone helping runaways can be fined a thousand dollars and put in jail for six months."

Angelina jumped in. "It's a stupid law. We act on higher authority in Michigan."

Emily rolled her eyes. "You mean that same higher authority that allows you to cheat the Indians out of their land? I've read my history. How can you people be so up in arms over one race and turn around and kill off another?"

"*We* didn't fight in the Indian wars, but you own slaves," Angelina stated.

"I do," Emily acknowledged. "Have you ever driven along the river?"

The girl narrowed her eyes suspiciously but nodded. "Of course I have."

"What did you see there?"

Angelina glanced at Helen blankly.

"Mills!" Emily exclaimed. "Tell me, sugar, how many people in your father's congregation work in the textile

83

mills?"

The girl opened her mouth but Emily burst out, "Those mills employ thousands of people, and they demand huge amounts of cotton to keep them running. Where do you think that cotton comes from? Northern industry depends on our slaves."

Helen crossed her arms and changed the subject. "Have you ever been to a slave market, Princess?"

Emily's father had never allowed her to attend an auction, but Sophia had. Emily chose not to believe some of the details as her friend tended to be overdramatic.

"Have you?" Emily reciprocated. "You've probably never left Michigan. What do you know of it?"

"I've heard firsthand accounts." Helen narrowed her eyes. "Angelina, I don't think our princess has any idea what kind of sludge her kingdom is built on. It's all been sanitized for her." She jabbed a forefinger at Emily. "You ask somebody who's been there. You find out what happens on the auction block. Then tell me what you think of your beloved slavery."

Emily's temper blazed. "I know what I've seen. We treat our people well. We feed and clothe them, give them housing and see that they get proper medical care. We even teach them the Holy Scriptures. In return, they work for us. They have a much better life under our care than they would in some backwoods shack eating 'possum and scratching a few crops out of the ground."

The bell above the doorway rang, ending the conversation, but Helen called out a parting shot. "The ones I've met would prefer a 'possum freely eaten over your richest cast-offs."

Mr. Marbliss smiled at them from the front of the room as the children settled into their seats. "I've graded your morning work and I'm very pleased. Jeremiah," he said to a small boy in the front row, "your reading and spelling are showing remarkable progress. And Emily, I can hardly believe you're the same student who came to me just a few weeks ago. Your skills in mathematics have improved so much."

Emily knew she owed that to Malachi Watson and his patient tutelage each night.

"Now get out your slates and we will practice our penmanship."

The afternoon passed slowly. Emily put the disturbing conversation out of her mind and worked steadily, knowing if she didn't put forth some effort her uncle would find plenty of undesirable ways to encourage her compliance.

***

Autumn turned crisp, and darkness fell earlier each evening. But every sunny afternoon found Emily on horseback. Coal Dust eased her homesickness and gave her a reason to tolerate the hours till school dismissed. At some point, her schemes to get sent home had dropped from memory like the colorful leaves that rained down with each gust of wind.

One Sunday afternoon Emily donned her riding habit and entered the stable. To her surprise, someone stood inside the mare's stall. "Hello?" she asked sharply.

A young woman whirled around. "You startled me!" she laughed.

Emily recognized her at once. "Miss Thatcher!"

The woman heaved a dramatic sigh. "Alas, yes, I'm still *Miss* Thatcher." Then her smile broke out again. "You must be the new groom daddy mentioned."

The new groom? Emily looked down at herself. Did she look like a groom? "I'm Mr. Milford's niece, from Carolina."

"Oh, how dreadful of me!" Melody exclaimed, not

looking especially sorry. "I am certainly glad to see you. I'm not at all sure I secured this saddle correctly."

Emily looked closer and sure enough, the woman had managed to pinch the mare's skin in the girth strap. Emily loosened the cinch. "Haven't you ever been taught how to do this correctly?"

The woman brushed the comment away. "Mr. Milford always insists on doing it for me. He's such a gentleman."

"Well, he's not here today. And it isn't difficult to learn. Watch." Emily refastened the strap, calling out instructions as she went.

"Thank you ever so much, dear," Miss Thatcher gushed when Emily had finished. "I'm sure I can do it now."

Emily had her doubts but she kept them to herself. Instead she asked, "Why don't you board Coal Dust at your own place? Your father has a large stable."

"I could, of course," Melody replied, shooting her a sly glance. "But when would I ever see your darling uncle?" She flashed Emily a brilliant smile and led the mare out of the stall. "Now if you'll pardon me, sweetie, I've been invited to tea."

***

Twice more Emily ran into Melody Thatcher in the barn, and twice more she had to resaddle the mare. But as the weather turned increasingly cold and rainy, Emily's outings with Coal Dust grew shorter and less frequent. More often she would pull up a chair in front of the lobby fireplace and read. Occasionally she'd try to recreate scenes from home with her watercolors, but they never turned out quite as sharp as her memories.

The first snow fell in mid-November, a fluffy white dusting that soon melted. Fall and winter leapfrogged for another month, but winter eventually established its authority. Snow that once sugared buildings and tidied dirty roads now choked them, leaving drifts three feet high, stopping traffic and deterring travelers. December became a white beast that locked the city in its teeth and froze the very air with its breath.

One blustery afternoon Emily curled up before the lobby fire to reread Sophia's penny novel, but when her uncle sat down at the piano she tossed it aside and soaked in the familiar melodies. After about thirty minutes, Isaac concluded with his favorite, "Moonlight Sonata," and retired to his office among a smattering of applause. Emily could see him through the door's open top and suddenly remembered the strange journal.

Her curiosity aroused, she strained to see exactly what he was writing on, but she couldn't make it out. She needed an excuse to enter the office and speak with him, and one quickly came to mind. One that had been plaguing her anyway.

She leaned on the half-door. "Uncle Isaac, have you ever been to a slave market?"

He looked up, surprised, and closed his book. She couldn't say for sure if it was the journal or just some ledger. "Yes," he said shortly.

"What's it like?"

His eyes narrowed. "You've never been?"

She shook her head.

He stuffed the book beneath a stack of papers and picked up something else. "I'm not the one to tell you about it. Ask Julia."

When it was clear he intended to say nothing more on the matter, she entered, tripping over a bag of apples. She kicked them aside. "May I borrow a book? I'm dreadfully bored with mine."

He glanced up briefly. "Help yourself."

She browsed through the horrid titles, keeping her eye on the stack of papers, and finally decided on *The Complete History of the Great Lakes Region*. She carried it over to the desk and stuck it under her uncle's nose. "Is this one any good?"

She pretended to bobble the book, and when it toppled to the desk it disrupted the stack of papers, revealing the book hidden beneath.

It was the journal.

"Oops, sorry."

He picked up the heavy volume and handed it back to her. "Yes, it's excellent if you're interested in that sort of thing. But it doesn't strike me as something a young girl would want to read."

She pretended to consider it, then reshelved the book. "You're probably right. I'll find something else."

But instead, she racked her brain. Why did her uncle hide the journal? What did the strange entries mean? And how could she get her hands on it again?

That evening after dinner Isaac stepped into the kitchen to lend a hand with cleanup, but Julia placed him at the table with a cup of coffee. "You jus' set and keeps out o' de way, Mr. Isaac. Dey's too many bodies in my kitchen a'ready."

Isaac stretched his arms behind his head and chuckled. "I can't argue with the chief. Now what did I do with my newspaper?"

Emily had seen it in his office that afternoon. "I'll fetch it!" she exclaimed, knocking a textbook from the table in her haste.

She closed both office doors carefully and rummaged beneath the scattering of papers on top of Isaac's desk. As she suspected, the journal was no longer there. Running her hand beneath the desk where the panels came together, she felt around for some means to open the secret compartment, but only a smooth surface met her fingertips. Pulling aside the chair, she lit the lamp and crawled beneath the desk, searching the wood for some irregularity, but her examination was in vain. In the end, the mechanism eluded her.

Disappointed, she blew out the light. The journal was so close!

She replaced the lamp and grabbed up the newspaper. As she left, she spotted a bolt of gray woolen fabric leaning against the wall beside the apples she had tripped over earlier. Her uncle collected the strangest items.

She returned to the kitchen just as Malachi tossed the pan of dishwater into the backyard and hung the tub on its hook. Then he picked up the burlap sack that always hung beside it and went out the swinging door to the dining room. Emily dropped the paper on the table before her uncle.

"Ah, thank you, dear," Isaac said, flipping it open.

Shannon came up behind him and planted a kiss on his cheek. Emily grimaced.

"I'm going home a little early tonight," Shannon said, pulling on a wrap. "My nephew has taken ill and I want to get back to check on him."

"Nothing serious, I hope?" Isaac asked.

"I don't think so. But my sister has had a difficult time taking in laundry and managing all those kids since her husband died. I just think I should be there to help."

Julia called from her place at the stove, "I gots jus' what a sick young'un needs. Zeke, grab dose buckets. I made too much chicken soup tonight." Julia was usually the model of thrift.

The black woman handed a bucket to Shannon as she went out the door. "Take one o' dese extra loaves, too. With some food in his belly, dat chil' should be hisself again in a few days."

"Thank you, Julia," Shannon said. "My sister will be

so grateful."

After Shannon left, Julia pulled a chair next to the stove and set her knitting on her lap. Emily joined her at the edge of the warmth, rubbing her arms. "Is it this cold all winter?" she asked.

Julia cut her eyes up at her. "Chil', you gots no idea what you's in fo'."

Isaac looked up from his paper. "That reminds me, Julia, I picked up some fabric at the market yesterday. Do you know anyone who might need a warm wrap?"

The woman glanced at him. "I's pretty certain I can fin' someone."

"Then use it to make whatever is suitable. I have no talents in that area. Emily, will you fetch it for her? It's in my office."

Emily rolled her eyes. He could have thought of it two minutes sooner. She pushed through the swinging door again, passing Malachi on his way back in.

The bolt of cloth still stood propped against the wall. Emily picked it up then stopped abruptly. The apples were gone.

She carried the material back to the kitchen. Malachi was gone, too, and so were the extra loaves of bread and the second bucket of soup. Julia must have sent the boy after Shannon. After all, her sister did have seven children.

Julia mistook her survey for uncertainty. "Jus' set it dere by the door to my room, please."

Emily put the matter out of her mind, joining Zeke and her uncle at the table. After only ten minutes of reading, she slammed the book closed and went to stand against the warmth of the stove. In the firelight, Julia's needles flashed back and forth, in and out, like an intricate dance. Emily watched, fascinated. "Could you teach me to do that?"

Julia looked at her uncertainly. "It takes practice and patience."

"I want to learn," Emily insisted. Perhaps it would help fill the long evenings.

"A'right, come set over here."

Emily pulled up a chair, and Julia explained how to wrap the yarn and draw it between the needles. Emily tried a few hesitant stitches, and Julia had helped her complete most of a row when Malachi stomped in the back door and hung the empty sack on its nail. He sat beside Zeke and soon the low sounds of the alphabet rose from the table as the old man painstakingly blended words from the Bible he used as a text.

"Sounds good, Zeke," Isaac praised him. "You're learning fast." Then he slid a section of the paper across the table and tapped a forefinger on it. "Why don't you try this?"

Zeke glanced at Malachi and the boy nodded. "Give it a try."

So the old man began reading in a slow, hesitant voice, pausing now and again for help from Malachi. "STOCKHOLDERS of the U.G.R.R. COMPANY hold on to your stock!!! The market has an upward tendency. Just today, fifteen thousand dollars worth of merchandise arrived on the express train, fresh and sound, from Kentucky. N.B. stockholders, don't forget the meeting today at 2 o'clock. All persons desiring to take stock in this prosperous company, be sure to be on hand. By order of the BOARD OF DIRECTORS."

Emily glanced over at the advertisement. It was similar to the one she'd seen on Isaac's desk her first day at the hotel. "Are you buying stock in a railroad?"

He shrugged. "Thinking about it. Be a good investment. This old hotel isn't too profitable, you know."

"But I thought you inherited your father's estate."

"Of course I did. But that was years ago."

Emily stared at him, waiting. He made it sound as if

there was hardly any of the fortune left. "But Mama said it was a beautiful estate, with thousands of acres and a hundred slaves. She said it was one of the finest plantations on the Carolina coast."

"And so it was," he stated.

Emily wondered about his failure to elaborate. Where had his fortune gone? Was he such a poor businessman? Or, and her eyes widened, was he a gambler? Had he squandered it all? He was often gone in the evenings. She wondered if her mother knew.

He skillfully turned the conversation. "I think large plantations will eventually become a thing of the past. Slave labor isn't really free, and cotton and tobacco wear out the land." He sighed. "But the South won't give it up until there's nothing left—or until it's wrested from their hands." He opened his paper, reciting in a somber voice:

"Thou, too, sail on, O Ship of State!
Sail on, O UNION, strong and great!
Humanity with all its fears,
With all the hopes of future years,
Is hanging breathless on thy fate!"

Chapter Eleven

The next day, Isaac met Emily at the door when she came home for lunch. "Emily, Shannon's nephew is worse, and she couldn't make it in this morning. Julia is swamped trying to do the work of them both. Would you mind skipping your afternoon classes to lend a hand?"

Skip school? She didn't hesitate a moment. "Of course not!"

"Good. I'm on my way to fetch the doctor. Julia can tell you what to do."

The woman pushed into the room with an armload of dishes just in time to hear the exchange. "When you's done eatin', you takes de linen off de line," she ordered. "Me an' 'Zekiel will finish up lunch." She dropped the dishes beside the wash tub, filled another plate, and disappeared into the dining room.

Ezekiel passed her coming in.

"Is it busy today, Zeke?" Emily asked.

"No more'n usual, miss."

Emily made herself a sandwich and took it to the table with a glass of milk. Halfway through the meal, Malachi burst through the door with his usual aplomb. Julia set on him at once. "Malachi Watson, when you gonna learn ta open dat door like a Christian 'stead o' like some heathen outta de brush?"

"Sorry, Mama," he cringed, shooting Emily a look of chagrin.

But Julia was too busy to send him outside to practice his faith proper. "See dat you get de chamber pots cleaned in rooms six and four. Den Mr. Isaac has a mess o' wood out back needs splittin'."

After bringing in the freeze-dried laundry, Emily got her first lesson in ironing sheets. She had grown accustomed to hard work, and if she didn't exactly find pleasure in it, at least it had gotten easier. She had, however, purchased a new pair of white gloves and wore them in public to cover her hands, which were becoming as red and calloused as Shannon's.

Julia placed three heavy flatirons on the stove to heat and then padded the kitchen table with an old blanket and spread out one of the stiff linens. When it was hot enough, she wrapped a rag around the handle of the first iron and pressed it across the sheet. The cloth softened and the wrinkles disappeared like magic. When the iron cooled, she replaced it on the stove and grabbed a new one.

"Now you try it."

Emily did it just as the woman had shown her, but instead of gliding smoothly along the top of the sheet like a duck on a pond, she pushed the whole mess across the table, blanket and all.

"No, no," Julia admonished impatiently. "You's not carvin' a turkey with it. Push it along gentle, like you's strokin' a horse."

The woman straightened the cloth and Emily tried again. At first she seemed to create more wrinkles than she removed, and she managed to burn her fingers twice, but after two or three attempts, Julia left Emily alone and began tossing ingredients for supper into a big black pot.

They were alone in the kitchen, but Emily ironed and

folded three more sheets before she worked up the courage to ask the question foremost on her mind. "Julia, have you ever been to a slave auction?"

The black woman stiffened, and silence iced the room like freezing rain. When she turned to meet Emily's eyes, her back was poker straight, her chin jutted out and her face was tight and proud. She looked like one of the African princesses in the folk tales Lizzie used to tell when they were little. "Why you wanna know?"

"I just wondered if the things I heard were true. My father never let me attend one, and when I asked my uncle about it, he told me to talk to you."

Julia turned back to her pot and remained silent so long Emily didn't think she would answer. Then her voice came low. "It all true. Everythin' you heard, it all true."

She worked the spoon, stirring memories. "I's born on a small farm in Georgia. Weren't so bad. Mr. Peters a hard man, but he lef' us alone if we gib him no cause to beat us. All dose years I had Mama and Daddy, my sister and brothers, a few other slave chil'ren to play with. I's happy enough. Din't know no better.

"Come a day Mr. Peters decide to sell out and head west. He put all us slaves on de block to sell piecemeal."

She stirred harder, clanking a rhythm on the side of the pot. "We was put in chains and marched up one at a time fo' de white men to examine, jus' like dey was buyin' beef cattle. Dey pinch my arms, poke at my ribs and pry open my mouth to look at my teeth. I's only thirteen, my body just learnin' to be a woman, an' I had to stand dere wearin' nothin' but my pride. But dat weren't de worse of it. I'd a stood dere all week if it keep my family together."

The stirring stopped and Julia stared into the pot. "I seen my daddy's face as his family was sold away. It a terrible thing for a man to be powerless. God gib him de job to look after his family, and de white man, he take it away.

"It kill 'im. He sol' away south and we heard later he jus' up and died. He only thirty-five years old.

"Mama, I don't know what happen to her, but I can still hear her scream like when dose babies bein' wrenched outta her arms."

The spoon clanked again. "I's lucky; my brother sol' wid me."

Emily absorbed the story in silence, and Julia cast her a dark glance. "Now you sees why I gots no tolerance for yo' high and mighty ways, yo' Southern talk and yo' petty orders. Picture yo'self on dat block, missy."

Emily's eyes grew wide. "But I'm white!"

Julia shook her head. "You's so full o' yo' own color you can't trade places wid a black person even in yo' own imagination. But when we's hurt, we bleed de same color, Miss Emily." She dropped the spoon and picked up a paring knife, flicking her fingertip with the sharp point.

"Look here," she demanded, shoving the drop of blood before Emily's eyes. "When we's hurt, you and I, we both bleed red."

***

That night, Isaac came home angry. "The best doctor in the city won't treat an Irish boy." He shrugged off his coat and hung it on a nail by the back door. Emily and Malachi glanced at each other over the open math book between them. "I had to settle for some idiot who prescribed sawdust and fish oil, or some such nonsense. It's clear the boy has scarlet fever. He has a purple rash and he's burning up. I'd like to wring that old fool's throat!"

Julia commanded, "Malachi, run an' fetch Doc Ferguson."

The black doctor confirmed scarlet fever. The child's home was quickly placed under quarantine and fixed with a bold red placard prohibiting anyone from entering or leaving. Within a week the disease had spread to three other children. Shannon's sister wore herself to exhaustion and finally came down with it, too. Shannon had to quit her job at the hotel to care for them all.

Isaac and Malachi brought them leftovers on several occasions, leaving the food outside the door, and Julia took in much of the laundry that comprised the family's income, adding it to her own workload. But everyone was careful not to violate the quarantine and spread the deadly germs.

Isaac sat at the kitchen table, his haggard eyes peering between the fingers pressed against his face. His hair stood on end from running his hands up and over his head.

"Emily, you've been a tremendous help this week, taking over Shannon's responsibilities, and I thank you. Business always slows in winter, but if it doesn't, I'm going to have to hire someone to take her place. I can't ask you to miss several weeks of school."

Several weeks? Emily perked up. Shannon was going to be gone for several weeks? Maybe this was the opportunity she'd been hoping for. Without the maid always underfoot, maybe Isaac would forget his foolish plan to marry her. Maybe...

Yes, she definitely had a plan.

Chapter Twelve

Yet another muffler was taking shape under Emily's hands. In only two weeks she had completed ten of the darn things. Sometimes she regretted asking Julia to teach her, but when darkness fell at five o'clock in the afternoon, there wasn't much else to do.

The household had taken to gathering around the stove during the long, snowy evenings. Sometimes Isaac pulled out a copy of William Cullen Bryant, or Tennyson, or Keats, but mostly he read Longfellow, and Emily became acquainted with the great Indian chief, Hiawatha, and with fair Evangeline, the Canadian maiden evicted from her homeland and separated from her bridegroom. She found herself concentrating on the versed stories, even identifying with the poor, banished maiden.

But tonight Isaac stared at his book vacantly, not turning pages, hardly even moving. Suddenly he slapped his cup of coffee down, sloshing it on the table. "A Christmas tree!" he exclaimed. "I am going to cut down a Christmas tree!"

Emily glanced out the window doubtfully. Nothing could be seen but wind-driven snow that flashed across the light of the window. She turned her eyes on him questioningly.

"Tomorrow, of course. For Shannon's nieces and

nephews. A tree would be just the thing to bring them some holiday cheer!"

Julia harrumphed, setting down the gray garment taking shape under her needle. "You spread too much cheer and you gonna be spreadin' germs as well. Mr. Milford, you get arrested if you go in dat house."

"Who said anything about going inside?" Isaac smiled at Emily and Malachi. "What do you say? Shall we bring them a tree?"

"Let's do it!" Malachi shouted.

Emily was slower to answer. Her compassion struggled to rise above the snowdrifts.

"Emily?" Isaac prompted.

Malachi answered for her. "'Course she wants to go. She's been clacking those needles together till I can hardly stand it."

"Malachi Watson," Julia admonished. "Miss Emily ain't a'clackin' no needles. She knittin' warm clothes for dem what gots none."

Malachi gave Emily's work a doubtful glance. "A fellow would have to be freezing to death before he put on that muffler."

Emily wadded the scarf into a ball and threw it at Malachi, needles and all.

"You hush!" Julia admonished. "She gettin' better all de time."

"Well I should be. There's nothing else to do when the weather's so blasted—" a quick peek at Julia "—uh, blessed cold. Who wears all these things anyway? Seems I've knitted enough scarves to wrap every neck in Detroit."

"Dey gets put to good use," Julia said firmly. "Tomorrow I'll show you how to make mittens."

"Tomorrow she's helping us get a tree," Malachi countered. "Aren't you?"

"All right," Emily relented.

Isaac grinned. "In that case, we're going to need some decorations. Julia, would you pop us some corn? The rest of us can search for ribbons, buttons, and scraps of bright cloth, anything to dress up the branches and bring a sparkle to some little eyes."

Emily raided her supply of hair ribbons and cut the lace edging off the cuffs and bottom of her traveling suit. Isaac tore an old flannel shirt into colorful strips to tie into bows. Even Zeke donated a pair of faded handkerchiefs. By the time the corn was popped, they had filled a bucket with pretty decorations. Then they spent the rest of the evening munching popcorn and stringing it into long garlands.

After breakfast the next morning, Isaac appeared with an ax and a length of rope. "Julia, do you think you could find Emily some appropriate clothing while I hitch up Barnabas?"

When Emily climbed in the sleigh beside Malachi, she was covered in so many pairs of woolen socks, woolen undergarments, woolen shawls, mittens and mufflers that she felt indebted to a whole flock of sheep. She practically rolled onto the seat, yet the icy air still found her skin.

Isaac tucked a fur robe over their laps and drove out of the yard, guiding Barnabas down roads packed firmly with use. The sleigh runners whisked over the snow with a soft whisper, and the bells on the harness jangled merrily. The sun set the world to sparkling as they moved quickly between buildings capped with snow and laced with jagged icicles.

They traveled the route that Coal Dust had carried her all those weeks ago, following Michigan Avenue through a countryside softened by a feathery white covering. It looked so different in winter that Emily scarcely recognized it, though she did know the bridge and the field where Coal Dust had bolted. With all the leaves down, she could even see a cabin in the copse of trees looking as mean as the old fellow with the shotgun.

A short way beyond, Isaac turned onto a narrow road that passed through a wood. The bare, gnarled fingers of hardwood trees splayed against the gray sky, and evergreens listed under the weight of their snowy skirts.

Isaac drove the horse into a clearing. "I own a dozen acres in here. They provide me with maple syrup, beechnuts, and firewood, and now they will offer up my first Christmas tree since I was a boy. Everyone out! Help me locate a good one."

Malachi trotted off into the woods. Isaac followed more slowly, and Emily dragged behind, stepping carefully in her uncle's tracks. The snow was deep and she was freezing. She remembered with longing the mild winters in Charleston.

Suddenly a great gob of snow smashed into her cheek, spraying her clothing and dripping down between the layers at her neck. She looked around in surprise. Isaac still marched steadily in front of her, but Malachi was nowhere to be seen.

"Malachi Watson, you're going to be sorry!"

Another snowball burst against her shoulder. This time she caught sight of the boy slipping behind a tree. She veered from the trail and bounded through the snowy drifts.

Malachi got off one more shot before Emily rounded the tree and slammed into him. They both fell to the ground. Malachi tried to roll away, but Emily heaped snow on him, rubbing it onto his face and neck. Soon they were both winded and laughing, and looking very much like the snowman the students had made in the schoolyard.

Malachi paused to dig snow out of his ear. "You know, for a girl, you tackle hard."

She grinned. "You forget I have a big brother."

Isaac was nearly out of sight among the trees. They raced to follow him, Emily no longer caring about the snow packing into her shoes and clinging to her socks.

When they caught up, Isaac was circling a tree about his own height, admiring it from all sides. "What about this one?" he asked them.

It was a pretty little tree, straight and even and fragrant. It would look beautiful in Shannon's yard dressed for the holiday. Emily smiled and nodded, and Isaac began chopping through the trunk.

As they waited, Malachi climbed a stump a few yards away. Spreading his arms, he toppled backwards like a falling tree. Then he flapped his arms and legs as though he hoped to fly away.

Emily giggled. "What in the world are you doing?"

"Haven't you ever made a snow angel before?"

"A what?"

"A snow angel!"

He jumped up and pointed to the shape left in the snow, a figure with outspread wings and a flowing robe. "It's the only way I'll ever look so pearly white," he grinned.

She considered the angel, her brow furrowed in thought. "Malachi, do you suppose there are black angels?"

"'Course there are."

"How do you know?"

"Everyone knows about the angel choirs, right?"

She nodded.

"Way I figure, God wouldn't even stop and listen if they didn't have at least a few black members."

Emily laughed and flopped in the snow to make her own angel. Overhead, the clouds tumbled like scraps of paper in a breeze. She no longer felt the bite of winter. In fact, she had grown uncomfortably warm beneath all her woolen layers.

"If you two are ready, the tree is already tied to the sled." The call sounded thin and far away.

Emily rose and threw one more handful of snow at Malachi, catching him on the cheek. He swiped it off and hollered, "Race you!"

Back at the sleigh, Isaac had cut several pine boughs that he laid on the floor at their feet. "I figure we might as well do some decorating of our own," he explained and turned Barnabas toward home. Then he began singing a song Emily had never heard before. "Jingle bells, jingle bells, jingle all the way…"

The children caught on quickly and joined in on the last few choruses. Emily's face tingled from the cold, but under the lap robe she was warm and cozy as they moved from one Christmas carol to another. They were still singing when they pulled up in front of Shannon's house.

The family lived in a shabby row house, and Emily couldn't imagine how nine people fit in the tiny building. As Isaac nailed two flat slabs of wood to the bottom of the evergreen tree, smiling faces appeared in the front window. Three of the children had hair in shades of red, but the littlest one, a freckle-faced boy with his face pressed to the glass, was blond as corn silk.

Isaac set the tree upright. "All right you two, help me dress this beauty up."

Together they tied on decorations. Emily fussed with the bows and draped the strands of popcorn in even waves. When they were done, the buttons glittered and the bright cloth blazed against the snow. The tree brightened up the whole drab street.

Isaac called to Malachi, "Help me move it so the others can see it from their beds."

When the tree nearly leaned against the glass, they piled back into the sleigh. Even before the horse moved, a pair of chickadees landed in the top branches and began pecking at the strand of corn. Emily smiled at the birds, and at Malachi and her uncle, and at the faces in the window, glad she had chosen to participate in the fun.

The three of them made merry again on their way home, but when they pulled into the hotel drive, all the jolly left Malachi's face.

And then Emily, too, caught the sound of a baying bark.

Chapter Thirteen

"Hello, Jarrod," Isaac greeted as he stomped his boots off inside the door. "One of your clients lose something again?"

"To be sure," Mr. Burrows answered, rising from a fireside chair to shake Isaac's hand. "It's the only thing that could induce me to share one of your godforsaken winters."

He caught sight of Emily. "Ah, Miss Preston, it is indeed an honor," he said, bowing over her hand. "I was hoping you were still in residence. Will you be joining me for dinner this evening?"

Emily glanced hopefully at her uncle. He gave her a cautionary look then nodded.

She turned to Mr. Burrows with a beaming smile. "I will. And perhaps you'd be so gracious as to grant me details of our beloved South. I've been away so long."

He bowed again. "It would be my pleasure."

"You boys want your same rooms?" Isaac asked, slipping behind the large desk.

"Already taken care of. You're man Zeke is a fine fellow." He dropped his voice, out of hearing of the hotel's other guests. "Old as he is, he'd fetch a fair sum."

Emily's smile faltered just a bit. She couldn't imagine sending away the grandfatherly old man.

105

Isaac waved Mr. Burrows off. "He's far too valuable for that. Let me get you a room key."

"Like I said, all taken care of. My boys are already sleeping off the effects of our travel. I simply want to sit beside this fire and soak up as much warmth as I can before I must go out again."

Emily chose to focus on the upcoming meal. She regained her smile and took the opportunity to make a graceful exit. "If you'll excuse me, I'd like to peek in on dinner."

Mr. Burrows nodded at Isaac. "Few more years and she'll make a fine plantation mistress."

Emily overheard him and his words brought her up short. She flipped her hair with annoyance. Did everyone expect her to marry?

Malachi met Emily in the kitchen, his eyes as dark as coal. "What's he doing here?"

"What you think he doin'?" Julia snapped. "Some black folks tryin' to be free this Christmas. He gonna drag 'em back in chains."

Emily cleared her throat, suddenly uncomfortable. "I won't be serving this evening. Mr. Burrows has asked me to join him for dinner and Uncle Isaac has agreed."

Julia met Malachi's eyes over Emily's head, and the slap of that look made Emily cringe. Her emotions warred inside her, but pride won out. Mr. Burrows was a fine, cultured gentleman and she would dine with him, no matter what they thought.

She raised her chin and looked Julia square in the eye. "I just want to see that dinner is prepared extra special tonight."

Julia's face grew stony, and her eyes burned into Emily's. Emily felt the heat rising in her cheeks and whirled from the room before the black woman could see it.

The evening passed pleasantly. Mr. Burrows was as agreeable as she remembered. His soft drawl and conversation centered on home made her happily forget all about her friends eating in the kitchen.

After dinner, her uncle entertained them with music. Mr. Burrows commented, "You play as well as my mother. She's always liked that last one. Bach, is it?"

"Beethoven," Isaac replied. "'Moonlight Sonata.' It has special meaning for me."

"Yes, yes, Beethoven. I never could keep all those German fellows straight."

The slave catchers stayed with them three days, keeping odd hours. They would suddenly appear or disappear, sometimes taking the dogs, often staying out half the night. Twice Emily heard them clomping up the stairs long after midnight.

The usual evening gatherings in the kitchen became particularly strained. She couldn't endure Malachi's frank gaze or Julia's scornful glare, so like a naughty child she retreated to the lobby with the guests.

On the night before Christmas, however, the three Southerners were absent all day, and the entire household set aside their differences, exchanging small gifts in front of the lobby fire before the work of the busy holiday began. Isaac read the Christmas story and led them in carols around the piano.

After the second stanza of "Hark! The Herald Angels Sing," the front door opened. "Milford!" boomed a voice that Emily recognized. "Got a delivery here from my daughter. She wanted to come but she's feeling poorly. She asked me to give this to your niece."

William Thatcher, the fat mill owner, thundered into the room with a small, brightly wrapped package. "She here?"

Isaac gestured to Emily, who was trying to sink into the couch once again.

"Hmmm. Ain't growed much yet. Here." He tossed

the gift in Emily's lap.

Inside, she found a beautiful china horse that looked exactly like Coal Dust. "Thank you," she mumbled.

He nodded. "I'll tell her you loved it."

"Wait," she said, jumping up. "I have something for her." She ran to her room and pulled out pen and paper. Here was her chance to try out her plan. Hastily, she wrote:

Dear Miss Thatcher,

Thank you for the beautiful horse. I will treasure it, though I must neglect its real-life likeness temporarily. Shannon has left us and we are all swamped with responsibility. My uncle, especially, is suffering her loss. I hope some young lady soon steps forward to fill the vacancy.

Thank you again, and may the holidays find you soon well.

Sincerely,

Miss Emily Preston

It was brief, truthful yet deceptive, warm yet matter-of-fact. And if she had judged the young woman correctly, it would produce exactly the desired effect. She delivered the letter promptly.

Mr. Thatcher tucked it in his vest pocket and boomed, "Milford, what are you doing about—?"

But his question was interrupted by a shout and loud stomping on the porch. The door burst open and Mr. Burrows entered. Behind him, his two companions ushered in an injured black man. They kept their guns pointed in his direction even though his wrists were bound with iron and he shivered uncontrollably with cold.

Mr. Burrows grinned jovially. "We'll be checking out."

Isaac nodded and rose from the piano.

Emily's stomach wrenched at the sight of the captive. The side of his head was sticky with blood that hadn't yet crusted in his wooly hair. One eye was swollen shut, and his lip was split and bleeding. There was blood on his shirt as well, but Emily couldn't tell if it had dripped from above or if it marked another injury.

Mr. Thatcher beamed at the newcomers. "Good day, Burrows! You found your man!"

The slave catcher shook his head. "No, that one got away. No sign of him anywhere. But I recognize this fellow from posters out of Georgia. He'll bring a tidy reward." He grinned again. "I think I'll buy my kids something extra special for Christmas this year."

Mr. Thatcher grunted. "Nasty business, slavery. But necessary, I suppose. Well, then, merry Christmas to you all!" And he strolled from the room, his question forgotten.

As Isaac tended to the paperwork, Julia drew the freezing captive toward the fire and dabbed at his wounds with a wet handkerchief. She disappeared momentarily and returned with a gray woolen coat which she fastened around his shoulders. Then she wrapped a knitted muffler around his head and neck. Emily recognized it as one of her own. Finally, she pulled two pairs of woolen socks over the man's raw, bare feet and slid them carefully into Malachi's boots.

The man had watched her without expression. Now he took her hand and a look passed between them as old as kindness and mingled with dignity and sorrow. He stuttered out something in a language Emily didn't recognize, though she thought she understood it.

It took only moments for the men to collect their belongings and leave, dragging with them the recaptured runaway and all of the afternoon's cheer.

Chapter Fourteen

The New Year roared in, and the business that marked the holiday traveling season faded away like memories of summer. The winter school term wouldn't resume for another week, and Emily was content to finish the chores set before her.

On a dim, gray morning when she could see her own breath if she strayed too far from the roaring fireplace, Emily worked at polishing the wood in the sitting room. As she rubbed vigorously, chilly even beneath a heavy shawl, Melody Thatcher swished into the room looking as fresh as a spring bloom and smelling strongly of lavender water. She carried a basket covered with a plaid cloth.

She rested her burden on the half door of Isaac's office and flashed him a beaming smile. "Mr. Milford, you never did come calling as you promised, so I had to take matters into my own hands." She dimpled prettily. "I brought you some cookies. I made them myself. Mrs. Beasly tried to help but I wouldn't let her."

"Miss Thatcher, this is a surprise!" Isaac exclaimed, setting aside his paperwork and joining her in the sitting room.

Emily smirked, not quite as surprised.

"And very thoughtful of you," he continued. "Thank

you." He took a small bite of one of the hard, round disks and set it down quickly.

Melody perched daintily on the divan. "This formality is so silly between such good friends. Please, call me Melody."

"All right, if you will call me Isaac," he smiled. "Would you care for some tea?"

"I would adore a cup, thank you."

Isaac caught Emily's eye and she nodded. When she returned with the tray a few minutes later, Melody was mid-sentence. "—have my sincere sympathies. And when I heard she left you understaffed, I thought the least I could do is offer my services."

"What services?" he wondered quietly.

The woman missed his slightly mocking tone. "Oh, I can do any number of things. I can greet guests—and serve tea!" she exclaimed, taking the tea tray jubilantly. "I'm sure we'll do just fine together. I've always liked your darling little hotel."

Isaac accepted a cup and sipped at the hot liquid carefully. "I appreciate your offer, Melody, but during the slow season, I'm afraid your talents would be wasted."

She touched his hand playfully. "Oh, nonsense," she said and guided him into a lively conversation. When her cup was empty she rose, and Isaac helped her back into her wraps. "Now, I'll come by tomorrow and no arguments," she stated and swept from the room, stopping to give Isaac a little wave at the door.

"What on earth dat be about?" Julia asked, coming from the kitchen.

Isaac stepped into his office. "Miss Thatcher must have heard that Shannon is away. She came to offer her help."

"Oh, lor'," Julia muttered, retrieving the tea tray. "If dat chil' come back, she gonna make mo' work fo' all of us."

Emily bit down her grin. Melody Thatcher was young, beautiful and wealthy, but she was certainly no maid. Perfect.

***

"Emily, I need to pick up some things at the dockside this morning. Would you like to ride along with me?"

Saturday was still young, but Emily had already cleaned three rooms. Now she was setting the dining room tables.

"Can I come?" Malachi asked.

Julia poked her head in from the kitchen. "Malachi Watson, you still gots to finish haulin' wash water fo' me. And then—"

"I'll fetch your water after I hitch up Barnabas," Isaac interrupted. "The kids need a little break. Maybe we'll even stop at Maynard's for pastries on our way home."

"Don't you go ruinin' yo' appetites now," Julia admonished, returning to her kitchen. "Lunch gonna be ready when you all gets home."

Emily glanced at the mantle clock. Ten forty-five. "Perhaps we should wait for Miss Thatcher," she suggested hopefully as they struggled into their wraps. Melody had arrived promptly at eleven each day that week, bringing with her an elegance and grace that Emily hadn't enjoyed since leaving home.

Isaac threw a look at the clock. "I really need to go now," he said with more haste than Emily thought necessary. "I have a package arriving this morning and I'd like to claim it before it gets misplaced."

Fresh snow softened hard edges and turned the city into a fairy world. Drifts overhung the tops of buildings and piled up like cotton along the road. Barnabas pulled them along the runner tracks, his breath frosting the air behind

112

him.

"Mr. Milford, how long is Miss Thatcher going to keep helping us?"

"Probably until Shannon returns, Malachi."

"How long will that be?"

"Oh, I don't know. Her family is getting better, thank goodness, and the quarantine has lifted. But scarlet fever is a long, slow recovery."

"I wish she'd come back. Miss Thatcher isn't good at much besides talking."

Emily bristled. "What's wrong with Miss Thatcher? She's charming, witty, and colorful. She makes all of us laugh. I like having her around."

Malachi rolled his eyes. "You just described a circus clown."

Isaac pulled up before the docks and tied Barnabas. "Don't go far," he called to them. "I'll be right back."

Emily and Malachi wandered to the water's edge. The river was a dark, cold, murky gray with a jagged fringe of frozen glass along its banks. Every now and again a chunk of ice floated downriver, broken off from the huge slabs piled up along Lake Huron's shore. But when ships could get through, they did. Even in the snow and cold, the docks bustled with activity.

"Emily, why don't you like Shannon?" Malachi asked, leaning against a crate.

"Who said I don't like her?"

"You don't fool me. I know you're hoping your uncle marries Miss Thatcher. I bet you even had something to do with her coming around all the time."

"She'd be an excellent hostess. A hotel must be hospitable, you know."

"She can't cook or clean. She's not suited for your uncle's way of life."

"And Shannon is?" she scorned.

"Yes!"

"Malachi Watson," she ranted, "my uncle is a blue-blooded Southern gentleman!"

"Emily Preston," he argued, "your uncle runs a hotel in Detroit!"

Emily whirled, turning her back on him.

Malachi sighed. "Don't you see? You're trying to do the very thing to your uncle that you don't want your parents to do to you. Mr. Isaac loves Shannon. You can't dictate his life to meet your expectations."

Isaac called to them and tied down a bulky package that clanged when it moved. "New tin ware," he said in answer to their unspoken question.

Emily regarded the large crate. It contained enough for four hotels.

"And a package of seeds," Isaac continued, pulling a small envelope from his pocket. "Shannon's always been partial to bluebells. Shall we go surprise her?"

Malachi looked at Emily pointedly. She sank onto the seat and unhappily crossed her arms.

***

"Spring cleaning? Mama, it's February!" Malachi protested.

"When de weather get warm, dese rooms gonna fill up with folk expectin' clean quarters. Ain't no better time to freshen 'em than when dey's standin' empty. Won't hurt you none to miss a week of school. 'Sides, Miss Thatcher comin' today. Gonna put dat girl to work.

"Miss Emily, I wants every scrap o' cloth outta de upstairs: curtains, rugs, blankets, spreads. Malachi, when she done, you move furniture so's we can scrub walls."

When Melody whirled in the front door, the hotel already smelled strongly of lye soap. At the same moment,

114

Isaac came downstairs toting a mattress to air on the porch.

"Isaac, what's going on?" she inquired.

Julia thrust a bucket into the woman's hands. "Spring cleanin'. Take dis upstairs. I want every fingerprint, every smudge, every piece o' dust outta dis house. Start wid de windows."

With a bewildered glance at Isaac, Melody carried the bucket up the staircase. Emily followed, desperate now to prove the young woman useful.

"Every window?" Melody asked doubtfully.

"It isn't as hard as it sounds," Emily encouraged. "Here, you just wring out the rag and wipe, see? And dry it with another cloth. Come on, try it."

With Emily's support, Melody managed to finish the first guest room. But as they moved on to the next one, she clasped her smooth hands together in dismay and went in search of Isaac. She found him cleaning ashes from the fireplace.

"I'm so sorry," Melody began. Emily could see her apologetic smile from the stairway. "I completely forgot I'm supposed to be at Mrs. Grace's house on Gratiot Avenue right now. She can't see anymore, poor dear, and I promised I'd help her write letters to her family this morning. I'm so sorry."

Isaac nodded graciously. "I understand. It's wonderful of you to help her."

Melody looked relieved. She smiled sweetly up at Isaac's sooty face as he helped her into her wrap. "I'll be back tomorrow," she promised with a cheery wave.

But she didn't return the next day, and the day after that Mr. Thatcher came to move Coal Dust into his own stable with the invitation to ride anytime. On the fourth day, as Emily surveyed the freshly mopped dining room with satisfaction, she heard the front door open. She turned to see Shannon's gentle smile.

***

Life fell back into routine so quickly it was as if Shannon had never left, and Emily had to admit Malachi was right. Shannon was better suited to the life her uncle had chosen. And she was as sweet as apple butter. Still, one stubborn corner of Emily's pride wouldn't accept the maid or the wedding plans she was busy fashioning.

One morning at breakfast Zeke sat reading his Bible, and Shannon leaned over his shoulder. "Ezekiel, I'm so proud of you for learning to read. I see you've found your namesake."

"Yes, miss," he said, reverently touching the page. "I always wanted to read the story I's named after."

"Well, what does it say?"

Zeke hesitated, looking around at the faces turning toward him expectantly. "I's jus' puzzlin' over dese verses in chaptah thirty-eight. It say, 'You will come from yo' place outta de remote parts o' de north, you and many peoples with you, all o' dem ridin' on horses, a great assembly and a mighty army; and you will come up against My people Israel like a cloud to cover de land.'"

Emily could feel a coldness start in her stomach and crawl down her arms and legs. She knew exactly what the old man was thinking. Once she had heard a slave singing such things on the plantation. It made her break into an icy sweat.

"You mean, you think the North is going to invade the South and free the slaves?" Shannon asked gently.

Emily's fear made her lash out in anger. "That's absolutely ridiculous!"

Isaac spoke up. "I hope it never comes to that, Shannon. War is a terrible business. The states must reach a peaceful agreement."

116

Zeke was quiet a moment, and when he spoke, his words were completely out of character. "Peaceful fo' whites, maybe, but black folk be sufferin' and dyin' while dey argue."

Emily was shocked. "How dare you say such a thing, Ezekiel! My family has treated you well!"

Zeke pursed his lips. "Ain't always so. It a hard thing to be a black man in de South. Maybe worse to be a woman."

Shannon turned kindly eyes on the old man. "Zeke, why do you stay at Ella Wood?"

Zeke chuckled. It was a dry, raspy sound. "I's seventy-eight years ol', miss."

Emily threw Shannon a look filled with all the scorn and rage she was feeling. "He stays because my mama *owns* him," she exploded.

"Actually, Emily," Isaac interrupted, "your mother doesn't own Zeke any more than she owns me. I gave Zeke his freedom fifteen years ago. He followed your mama to Ella Wood of his own free will."

Emily gaped at her uncle in disbelief. Then she rushed from the room, shoving Shannon roughly into a chair as she passed.

She didn't move quickly enough.

Isaac caught her just outside the swinging door, his face dark with rage. He grabbed her roughly by the arm and dragged her through the kitchen and out across the frigid yard, releasing her only after they had reached the privacy of the stable. He loomed in the doorway, as big as Apollo, and glared at her with all the fury of the ancient gods.

"If you ever treat Shannon that way again, you will not sit down for a week! Do you understand me?"

Emily flashed him a look of pure hatred.

"And I have had enough of this attitude of yours. What makes you better than Shannon? Better than Zeke?"

117

She threw back her head and focused all her contempt on him. "My father is William Samuel Jackson Preston III, owner of one of the largest plantations in all of Charleston County!"

"And what if that were all wiped away? What if your land was gone and your name meant nothing? What would make you better then?"

Her mouth opened in astonishment. "You're crazy! That can't happen in a million years!"

"Can't it?" he asked in a voice deadly calm.

"You don't believe Zeke's reading meaning into that prophecy, do you?" she scoffed. "His notion of Northerners riding in to free the slaves is absolutely ridiculous."

"Perhaps, but that's beside the point. I want to know where you get this idea that God created you a little higher than the rest of humanity."

She tossed her head. "I told you, I am the daughter of—"

"A pedigree?" he scorned. "Because your daddy has a number at the end of his name you have the right to cut down Shannon? Or to demand that Zeke fulfill your every petty wish? Or to show Malachi and Julia your disdain? I come from the same stock as you, sweetheart, and I can tell you Barnabas here has a nobler pedigree than we do. Under your fancy titles, you are just the same as everybody else."

Emily narrowed her eyes spitefully. "*Maybe* I could agree to equal status with Shannon, but Isaac Milford, even without my wealth and name, I would still be white!"

He was blocking the doorway, so she whirled around and showed him her back. And there, leaning against a pitchfork at the back of the stable and listening to every word, stood Malachi.

Chapter Fifteen

"Emily, spell 'dictation,'" Mr. Marbliss called from the front of the room.

Emily's gaze was fixed on the bare fingers of the maple tree across the street, though she didn't really see them scratching against the side of the bakery in the breeze. Nor did she see the baker walk outside and stand looking up at it with his hands on his hips. She did see the midnight black eyes of Malachi staring unflinchingly at her from behind the stall's half door. They were filled with something she couldn't define. Not hurt, exactly. More like a sad disappointment that rendered her arguments to her uncle as hollow as the squirrel hole in the tree outside. She'd only been able to hold his gaze a moment before fleeing past her uncle and out the barn door.

"Emily? Are you going to join our spelling bee?" Mr. Marbliss quizzed. "Emily!"

Her head jerked, and a few snickers jangled through the room. Someone, it sounded like Angelina, whispered, "Maybe she can spell 'distraction.'"

"I'm sorry," she answered, lifting her chin, "I didn't hear the word."

"It was 'dictation,'" he repeated, a warning in his tone.

She spelled it perfectly, but on her next turn she missed

"anyway," to the sound of more mockery. After that she did try to focus on her schoolwork, but it was hopeless. Her mind kept pulling itself back to yesterday and to the lead weight her heart had become.

That afternoon she avoided Malachi, walking a different route home from school, escaping for a long ride on Coal Dust, and taking her dinner to her room. She even managed to miss him as she rushed through her chores. But he knew her habits too well. He found her bundled on the front porch watching her breath freeze against the very last hint of sunset.

"Hi," he said, drawing his coat tighter around himself. He sat on the railing and leaned back against the house with one long leg propped in front of him.

She didn't answer, which brought to mind the one-sided conversations they used to have. He didn't say anything else for a long time, either. They just sat there watching traffic pass on the road. She began to shiver, wanting to return to the fire inside but unable to.

Malachi shifted on the railing. "Emily, you remind me of a wild thing trapped in a cage. I know how much you miss your home. You're drawn out here to this porch, looking away south, waiting to be set free."

A wagon rumbled by filled with a load of hay.

"You're not the only one waiting. There are others out there, trapped like you, looking to the North, drawn by the Candle Star." He leaned out over the railing till he could see the bright light over the roof of the hotel. "But they're held by chains."

He drew his head back under the porch roof and leveled her with a full, bold stare. "Emily, do you agree that God made us both, just like he made black and white angels?"

"Of course I do," she sniffed. "I'm no heathen."

"If you really believe that, you cannot justify any differences between us."

"Oh, yes I can. You and I are of completely different stations."

He scoffed. "Stations are man's own invention, based on pride and power. There's no natural basis for it whatsoever. We hurt the same. We love the same. Our only difference comes down to color. We're like two painted houses on the same street."

"Why are you telling me this? Why do you care so much what I think?"

"Because underneath that proud white skin you have determination and a good heart. I respect you for it and consider you my friend."

She looked away south. "Don't you have friends of your own race?"

He shrugged. "Of course I do. Lots of them. But not all of them understand me. I've been called a fool for holding your uncle—a white man—in high esteem. My dream to become a doctor—a white man's profession—has been called presumptuous. I'm straddling two worlds, and not everyone can comprehend that I'm trying to make things better. But you do."

Her head snapped around. "What do you mean?"

He stared hard at her. "I mean, you understand about breaking out of boxes, trying what everyone says is impossible. You're doing the same thing yourself; resisting your parents' plans, grasping for the opportunity to become an artist. Golly, come to think of it, I've seen you buck about every restriction placed on you!"

She frowned.

He continued more earnestly, "But even within these pressures, we can control who we become."

He looked up at the stars again. "Your uncle once said that poetry is art because it's bound beauty. Maybe people are like that, too. Maybe character is being able to find a

121

way to grow and develop into exactly what we were meant to become, even when we're crowded with limitations. Maybe," he paused a moment, reflecting, "maybe it's even the limits that push us to become extraordinary."

They sat together until complete darkness overtook the city and the rest of the stars popped out like jewels. Emily's teeth began chattering audibly.

"Emily, I'd like to take you to a meeting at my church tomorrow."

"But tomorrow's Saturday."

"It's a special meeting. There's someone I'd like you to hear."

Malachi stood up from the railing and stretched out his hand to her. "Come on, let's go inside."

Emily stared at the dark hand, the palm shaped just like her own, the flesh warm and alive and feeling just like her own, the fingers that struggled and grasped like her own. And she reached out and clasped it.

***

The next evening was cold and clear. Shadows were lengthening, but overhead the March sky still shone aquamarine. Malachi led Emily through the city to a beautiful, red-brick church with a steeply pitched roof, tall Gothic windows, and spires where the roofline met the building's face. Two smaller turrets perched on either side of a gabled entry so the entire facade seemed to point the way heavenward for those passing on Monroe Street.

Emily and Malachi weren't the only ones entering the church. A steady trickle of humanity streamed down both sides of the street and passed through the church's double doors. Inside, the sanctuary was a sea of black and white faces. The pews were full, and folks were beginning to crowd into the aisles. The two children jostled their way to a

122

front corner where they could just glimpse the podium over the flowers on the woman's hat in front of them.

"So this is where you go to school?" Emily queried, taking in the brilliant colors of the windows and the rich, dark wood of the pews. "It's a sight better than mine."

"We take pride in our church. It was started by Blacks the year before Michigan became a state, and it's grown steadily from there. This building was finished only two years ago." He raised one eyebrow at her. "Are you surprised?"

She didn't answer but continued to admire the beautiful facility.

"Emily," he said with a trace of impatience, "you've now spent seven months in the North. Do you really still think of free Blacks as a bunch of illiterate slaves? Look over there," he pointed, indicating a dark face. "Mr. Lewis runs a fine bakery. There's Mr. Lambert, the tailor who owns a prosperous clothing store. Up front, that's Mr. deBaptiste, the barber who owns the steamboat. Mrs. Willis, over there, is an excellent seamstress in demand by the richest folks in the city. We're an educated, important section of Detroit society, and," he added pointedly, "every slave on your father's plantation is capable of the same, given the opportunity."

Before Emily could form a response, there was a stirring on the dais, and the crowd grew still. An elderly black man with a presence of authority stood behind the podium.

"That's our pastor, Reverend Davis," Malachi whispered.

"Ladies and gentlemen, welcome to Second Baptist Church." The preacher's voice resonated in the large room. "We are deeply honored to host this gathering, and we are proud to have you stand with us before God and man to support the cause of freedom for every American. But before I introduce our speaker, let us beseech our Lord together."

123

As the reverend prayed, Emily peered out across the sea of faces and realized this was the dream Malachi worked for—black and white side by side; accepting, united and free. The preacher's words floated to the ceiling, low whispers hovered about the pews, and the vision of two races bowing equally before their Creator burned into Emily's mind.

"Our speaker needs no introduction to many of you," the preacher announced, "but he's worthy of our highest recognition. Please join me in welcoming the esteemed Mr. Frederick Douglass."

The room burst into a cannonade of applause as a tall, spare black man with a frizzle of hair just turning to gray shook hands with Rev. Davis and stood formally before the podium. His face, as he waited for the greeting to fade away, was at once dignified and self-assured, and he reminded Emily of an Old Testament prophet—one of those friends of God who brought a message for His people.

Mr. Douglass began to speak in a deep voice, one so gentle that it seemed soft, though it reached to every corner of the room.

"I come before you this evening with both elation and soberness of heart. Elation, because before me I see the success of a free Negro community. I see colored men and women who have proven they can thrive under the freedom granted to them. I see those who have risen from ignorance and debasement to intelligence and respectability.

"Tonight, I celebrate your achievements. I celebrate this beautiful church and this congregation of free Coloreds committed to the betterment of their souls and their community. But while we celebrate, let us address the prejudice that seeks to subdue our race and deny us the fullness of our liberty. Let us speak of the America that has neither justice, nor mercy, nor religion in the case of the Negro.

"What would the colored man ask of this America?

Only that, speaking the same language and being of the same religion, worshipping the same God, owing our redemption to the same Savior, and learning our duties from the same Bible, we shall not be treated as barbarians. We ask that the door of the schoolhouse, the workshop, the church, the college, shall be thrown open as freely to our children as to the children of other members of the community. We ask that the American government assure life, liberty and property to the colored American. We ask that justice be rendered alike to every man according to his works."

Mr. Douglass's words rose in volume and passion. "We ask that the cruel and oppressive laws, in both North and South, which deny citizenship to free people of color, shall be denounced as an outrage upon the Christianity and civilization of the nineteenth century. We ask that the complete and unrestricted right of suffrage be extended to the free Colored man, as it is to the white man. And finally, we ask that slavery be immediately, unconditionally, and forever abolished."

The auditorium burst into applause at these powerful, explosive phrases. Emily felt herself lifted on the eloquent words, as if she was soaring on a swift wind. For the first time she dared to let herself consider such ideas—ideas Malachi had been demonstrating all along.

When the applause died away, Mr. Douglass continued in a voice made low once again. "During our celebration of all we have accomplished as free Coloreds, despite America's reluctance, let us especially not forget those who have nothing yet to rejoice over. Let us remember those in bondage. Those who toil for the gain of another. Those who sleep in hovels so another might sleep in a mansion. Those who wear rags so that others may clothe themselves in silk. Those who live in ignorance that another may be educated. Those who labor under a burning sun so someone else may idle in leisure. Those who know hunger that another might feast. Those whose names may be enrolled in heaven, among the blest, but on earth must be recorded in the master's ledger, along with horses, sheep, and swine. Those who suffer whip, gag, pillory, chain, pistol and bloodhound.

"Slavery has long ravaged this nation, dating back to the landing of the pilgrims on Plymouth Rock more than two centuries ago. Now those few slaves have grown to number over three million, and this most dangerous institution threatens to tear the American Union apart.

"But even so, this is a period of activity and hope. Let us join together—black, white, man, woman, and child—to protest the evil that holds one man in bondage to another. With every avenue freedom makes available, let us demand justice where justice is long due." His voice rose in a crescendo and "amens" rumbled about the room.

Emily hung on the edge of the silence as the speaker paused. Then he delivered his prophecy with assurance and quiet strength, leaving no room for doubt in the minds of his listeners. "That Coloreds shall yet stand on an equal platform with our fellow countrymen is certain. Be assured that we shall see a final triumph of right over wrong, of freedom over slavery and equality over caste."

With this quiet declaration, the great man humbly, but with awesome dignity, took his seat on the platform while applause filled the sanctuary and spilled out into the city. Someone began singing a hymn, and the whole gathering took it up as an anthem. Even Emily joined in with the strong, confident strains:

> *Blow ye the trumpets, blow! The gladly solemn sound*
> *Let all the nations know, to earth's remotest bound:*
> *The year of jubilee is come!*
> *The year of jubilee is come!*
> *Return, ye ransomed sinners, home.*

Ye slaves of sin and hell, your liberty receive,
And safe in Jesus dwell, and blest in Jesus live:
The year of jubilee is come!
The year of jubilee is come!
Return, ye ransomed sinners, home.

The last reverberations of the verse died away, but Emily thought even the black and white choirs of heaven couldn't match the triumph and challenge that song sent forth into the darkness of that Detroit night.

Chapter Sixteen

Spring returned with a demonstration of color. Yellow daffodils poked their heads up along street borders, and spring violets appeared in boxes on a hundred different window sills. Cass Park reawakened with a green blush as soon as the melting snow seeped into the soil, and Shannon worked, in preparation for the wedding ceremony to be held there, to merge the River Street Inn with the display.

Spring also brought a letter welcoming Emily home.

On an afternoon in April, one week before the train would carry her back to her beloved Ella Wood, Emily climbed onto the front porch and leaned pensively over the railing where she had watched so many sunsets.

It wasn't that she didn't want to go home; leaving was just harder than she imagined it would be. The people here had fused into a sort of family—not one bound by blood, but one pieced together like a patchwork quilt. Each square was of a different cloth, a different color, a different pattern, and the result had grown warm and comfortable.

Julia came out on the porch carrying a rug which she shook over the rail. "Miss Emily, will you go fin' Shannon? She out back somewhere. Tell her we has a full house tonight and I need her to peel potatoes."

"Sure, Julia."

Emily found the maid digging in the garden's rose room. At her approach, Shannon sat back on her heels and breathed in the rich smell of damp earth. "I love spring-time," she sighed, "the renewal of life after snow."

"I'm just glad it's not cold." Emily sat at the wrought iron table observing the manicured room with distaste.

Since that emotional day in the kitchen, Emily and Shannon held to an unspoken truce. The maid was as gracious as ever but seemed cautious, seldom straying from safe topics. The easy manner she once displayed had evaporated like a pot boiled dry.

"We haven't seen the last of winter yet," Shannon cautioned. "It can still get downright frosty even into May."

"Julia sent me to tell you she needs potatoes peeled."

"Tell her I'll be there in a few minutes." She pulled out a few more weeds, clawing the soil loose with her hand rake. "I wish you could be here for the wedding, Emily, when the first roses bloom."

Emily had resigned herself to the marriage. In fact, she could even see how foolish she had been. She just didn't know how to tell Shannon. Instead, she wrinkled her nose at the rigid trellises staked into the ground, climbing with last year's spindly, leafless growth.

"Why don't you let the roses grow where they want to?" Emily asked.

Shannon drew a pair of large shears from the folds of her dress. "Because in a few years I'd have a big, ugly briar patch." She made a few snips at a vine, cutting off large sections that fell to the ground.

Emily's eyebrows lifted. "You're going to kill it."

Shannon smiled. "Roses need to be pruned to make room for new growth."

"But if you cut off all the branches, how will you get any flowers?"

"Old wood can grow rotten and diseased," the maid

patiently explained. "Cutting it off actually produces healthier growth and bigger blooms."

Emily grimaced. "But do you have to tie them up?"

Shannon laughed. "Miss Emily, roses are climbers. They want to cover the trellis. With a little guidance, they grow into strong, beautiful plants."

Emily watched the woman snipping and tucking, tending the flower bed like a mother devoted to her children. She shook her head. Even roses had rules.

"Stay and finish your flowers, Shannon," Emily said, rising. "I'll help Julia."

She scrubbed her hands and face at the pump in the backyard, wiping her hands on the seat of her skirt, then entered the kitchen and tied on one of Julia's aprons. After only four potatoes, Malachi burst through the door.

"You march right back outside, young man, and enter my kitchen like a gentleman." Julia's wooden spoon waggled a warning.

Malachi meekly obeyed.

Julia muttered, "Thank heaven his daddy can't see what a barbarian I raised."

Emily laughed as the boy entered a second time. "Won't you ever learn?"

He shrugged helplessly. "Mama, can I go fishing?"

"Not before dinner, you can't. I need wood chopped and hauled inside. Den I need you to help serve. But after dinner you's free. You takin' de Willis boy?"

"No, I figured I'd ask Emily since she's leaving."

"Den Miss Emily, after dinner you's free too."

***

The water flowed toward the west as though drawn by the orange, low-hanging sun. Across the river, the green field that was Canada seemed to burn in the fiery rays. Belle

130

Isle floated low in the water two miles to the east.

> "*River! that in silence windest*
> *Through the meadows, bright and free,*
> *Till at length thy rest thou findest*
> *In the bosom of the sea!*"

Malachi's voice rippled over the scene and Emily recognized Longfellow's tribute. Her uncle had read it to them a thousand times. The poem seemed to capture the beauty before her.

They settled on a vacant dock. "You ever go fishing before?" Malachi asked.

"Sure. My brother used to take me sometimes, if I could catch him in a charitable mood."

"Cultured Southern girls are allowed to fish?" Malachi asked, raising one eyebrow playfully. "I wouldn't have guessed it."

"Would I let that stop me?" she joked.

They fished in silence, the river swallowing up the colors of the setting sun.

"So what are you going to do when you get home?" Malachi finally spoke.

She knew what he was asking, and she had given it a lot of thought since their discussion at the state fair so long ago. Boxes, she decided, didn't have to be prisons.

"I'll follow my parents' wishes. I'll be charming, well-mannered, the belle of every ball. And," she cut him a sly glance, "I'll seek out every school of art I can find."

He grinned, his teeth white in his dark face. "That's the spirit!"

She shifted on the dock boards. "So what will you do when I leave?"

He shrugged. "Continue going to school and working at the hotel, I guess. Same as always." He cast his line

131

farther into the river. "I know nothing changes overnight, but sometimes it feels like nothing changes at all."

"Maybe it would change faster if I wrote to the medical school in Ann Arbor and ordered their recommended texts—to be delivered to the River Street Inn, of course."

Malachi's mouth fell open. "You could do that?"

"If I come home a proper young lady," Emily laughed, "my daddy will do anything I ask."

"Then I take back everything I just said about nothing changing, because you wouldn't have done that last fall."

She shrugged. "You're probably right."

Malachi sobered and Emily could tell he had something else on his mind. He started to speak, stopped, then started again. "Emily, where you're going, there are a lot more adjustments that need to be made than here."

She narrowed her eyes. "What are you getting at?"

"I'm just saying there may be things you can do."

"Me? I barely have control of my own life."

"Little things add up into bigger things."

"Malachi," she challenged, looking him in the eye, "I cannot wipe out slavery. Even talking about such a huge transformation terrifies me. Everything I know—everything I grew up believing..." her voice drifted away.

He nodded sorrowfully. "I know," he said. "Just look for the little things."

***

Warm, welcoming lamplight issued from the hotel's kitchen window, but Emily climbed the darkened porch steps. "Go on ahead," she urged. "I want to sit out here alone for a while."

Malachi collected her fishing gear and disappeared behind the house.

Emily leaned against the porch rail, looking away

south as the sky darkened and the stars grew brighter. Soon she'd be leaving for home, to a world as different from Detroit as China.

Would it take time for her to readjust? Would anything ever be the same? Could she do as Malachi asked?

The door opened behind her. "Ah, Miss Preston, I'm so glad I found you."

She turned around. In the dim light of the doorway, she could make out the outline and features of a man. "Mr. Burrows," she welcomed. "What a pleasure."

"Indeed," he returned, coming to stand beside her. "How was your winter?"

"Long and difficult, I admit. Detroit is nothing like home."

He pressed his hands down on the railing, gazing up at the crescent moon. When he spoke again, his voice had changed. It was thin and brittle, like the jagged skim of ice around a puddle on a chilly morning. "You couldn't have spoken anything truer. And that brings me to my proposition."

Emily's spine prickled. She didn't like his new tone. It recalled to mind the hard way he had left at Christmas, and she couldn't help but wonder at the fate of the captured man he had hauled away with him.

"A proposition?" She hesitated.

He faced her, and his features weren't pleasant to look at. She remembered the threats he'd left hanging last fall, the time he had returned, mud-spattered, to the yard.

"Every time I track my man to this city, I lose him. It's like that old magician's trick, place the rabbit in the hat and...presto! It disappears. But each time my rabbit vanishes, I lose money.

"You've lived here. You're part of the community. You go to church and to school. You must have seen things during your stay."

Emily wiped her suddenly damp palms down her skirt. "They treat me different," she hedged. "They know I'm not one of them."

Mr. Burrows turned back toward the street, leaning hard on the railing again. "But you have access to places I'll never be allowed into. All I ask is that you keep your eyes open. Take notice of details. Try to recall anything you've seen or heard that might help me find the holes my rabbits slip into. You're from a good, slave-owning family. Will you help me?"

Emily swallowed painfully. Jarrod Burrows was cultured and charming when he wanted to be, but she didn't like the way he was lumping them together. By accepting his offer, she knew she was taking part in the guns, the chains, the dogs, but she was too frightened to deny him. She nodded weakly.

Mr. Burrows smiled then, and the gentleman returned. "I knew I could count on you, my dear. It's certainly a pleasure to see you again." He bowed low over her hand and reentered the hotel.

Emily turned again to the south, but the beauty of the evening had grown dark.

Chapter Seventeen

The next morning Emily felt as transparent as a window pane. She went through the routine of eating breakfast, certain that Malachi and the others could read her duplicity. Instead of lingering in the kitchen until it was time to leave for church, as she did most Sundays, she escaped to her room to pack.

Her trunk was still in storage in the barn down the road, so she carefully folded her clothing and left it in neat piles on her bed. She wrapped some items she had collected during her stay—a few books, some lace from a shop window, the horse figurine from Melody Thatcher, an engraved pen, and a framed painting of her uncle's inn that she had finished only days before—to secure them for her journey, but the entire time she was dreading her inevitable meeting with Mr. Burrows.

Church left her feeling downright guilty. During the service, she could feel God watching her, frowning down on the deception she was living, but she couldn't figure a way to weasel out. No matter who she chose to please, she was bound to disappoint someone.

When the family arrived home, Mr. Burrows and his men were lounging in the lobby, their soiled clothing contrasting with the Sunday best of the others. Shannon slipped away to help serve the noon meal. Emily wished she could hide as easily, but Mr. Burrows rose and greeted them, addressing her specifically.

"Hello again, Miss Preston. What a lovely gown. It becomes you nicely. I hope you will pleasure me by wearing it to dinner. Isaac, she will be joining us, won't she?"

"Of course," her uncle conceded, catching her eye and communicating a stern warning. He needn't have bothered. "Malachi can serve today in her stead."

Emily looked down at the gown. It was her favorite, the one with the layers of fabric on the skirt and the lacy bell sleeves. She had kept it nice all these months, and its full skirt easily forgave her extra height.

Mr. Burrows turned to her. "Miss Preston?"

Emily dropped a curtsy, hoping her smile didn't wobble like her knees. "I'd be delighted."

"Excellent," he beamed. "Then my boys and I had best quit lounging and make ourselves presentable."

Emily thought his smile looked predatory. She knew he'd be pumping her for information, however delicately, and she felt like a canary in a cage with the cat sitting outside looking in. The strains of "Moonlight Sonata" follow her down the hall as she fled to her room.

The piles of clothing on her bed offered a perfect distraction. She scooped up as much as she could carry and hustled for the barn. As she passed through the lobby, her uncle never looked up from the piano.

The windows of the barn were so dusty they looked as if they'd been painted gray, so she left the door open to cut through the gloom. A sunbeam illuminated the wagon, and just beyond, in a corner, she spotted her trunk.

The barn felt cool and smelled musty, like a cellar in need of a good whitewashing. Thick bricks muffled the sounds of life carrying on outside the walls, and Emily could imagine when the daylight faded the building would feel unmistakably tomblike. The thought made gooseflesh break out on her arms, and she hastened to deposit her belongings.

The sudden flapping of a pigeon roosting under the eaves made her cry out. It let out a soft cooing, and she sagged against the trunk in relief. Mr. Burrows had her strung higher than a Thoroughbred mare. She couldn't let him get to her like this!

At that moment, the door creaked gently on its hinges behind her.

She stiffened.

A breath of sweet air swirled into the room, swaying her skirts and tumbling wisps of straw about her feet. Of course the same breeze had simply nudged the door open wider, but her nerves weren't acknowledging logic.

Emily locked her trunk and faced the door. It was slanted against the wall with room enough for someone or something to hide behind it. She was being silly, she knew, but if she didn't take a peek and set her imagination to rest, all manner of specters would follow her home.

She approached the door boldly, took hold and swung it closed.

Malachi suddenly jumped out and clapped a hand over her mouth. Emily's eyes bulged and a scream rose in her throat. She fought for breath.

"I'm sorry, Emily," the boy spoke softly, "but it's important that you don't draw attention to this building. Promise not to scream?"

She nodded, her eyes still huge.

He moved his hand and turned to close the door tightly.

"Why are you doing this?" Emily whispered, drawing clenched hands to her chest.

In answer, he pointed to the hay piled in the back of the barn where two forms huddled, frozen, under a small blanket. Two forms with black, terrified faces.

Sudden understanding dawned on her. Malachi was harboring runaways!

"The piano, that haunting song Mr. Milford always plays," he explained, "that's our signal that the barn is occupied. We try to keep folks away, but somehow you blundered in anyway. Now that you know, maybe you can help us."

"Help you?" she asked weakly. In how many directions could she be pulled?

Malachi leveled her with a frank gaze. "Emily, you are not the same person you were when you came here. You're deeper, kinder, humbler, and you understand about cages. I'm asking you to help me, to help my people, to help Abraham and Rachel."

Emily looked into his coal black eyes and recalled that magic night at his church; the night Mr. Douglass had made the impossible seem possible. She felt the stirring again in her heart, but it was one thing to listen to fine words being spoken from a podium. It was something else entirely to act on them.

He pulled her to where the runaways huddled, a girl and a boy, about the ages of herself and Malachi. Their faces were guarded, but they could not disguise their exhaustion. Nor could they conceal the hardship of their journey. It was written all over their tattered clothing and gouged into the soles of their bare feet.

But old ways die hard. Despite the eloquence of Frederick Douglass and her respect for Malachi, Emily couldn't help but wonder if she knew their master.

And what about Mr. Burrows? How could she hide this from him?

She opened her mouth to tell Malachi that she could not help him. And then she saw the wound.

The girl's leg stretched out beyond the edge of the

blanket, straight and taut. A dirty bandage wrapped around her calf muscle seeped with fresh blood.

Blood as red as her own.

She looked again into the girl's face, and this time she saw the shadow of a whip. She felt the wrench of hunger and the scorch of a burning sun. She heard the rattle of chains, felt their cold bite on her wrists. She could smell the stench of sweat and blood and fear.

For the first time she saw beyond herself. And she couldn't walk away.

"Burrows?" she asked.

Malachi nodded.

She remembered her own journey North, how terrified she had felt on the train, how unfamiliar the sights and sounds were. What if she'd had to travel all that way on foot? What if she had been without Zeke's protective guidance? What if she'd been pursued, and capture meant torture or even death?

The pair had traveled far. The river flowed only a few streets away. She could walk there in ten minutes.

She glanced back at the wound, at the red, red blood.

"I'll do it."

Malachi's words came low and urgent. "Be back this evening, just before dark. Use the alley door."

***

Emily arrived late to the dining room. A brief glance showed her uncle sharing a table with Jarrod Burrows and his two thugs. They had already been served plates of meatloaf with early lettuce and huge slices of crusty bread. She marched to the table. She knew what she had to do.

At her appearance, Mr. Burrows stood and pulled out the empty chair beside her uncle. "Miss Preston," he nodded, "I had begun to wonder if you took ill."

139

Though her hands shook beneath the tablecloth, she forced a beaming smile. "I'm sorry I'm late. I have acquired quite a collection of trinkets during my visit and I thought to pack them in the bottom of my trunk. But as my trunk is still out in the *barn*," she said significantly, "it took a little time."

Her uncle's head snapped up and he scrutinized her keenly.

"They are all *hidden away quite nicely*," she continued, "but I simply cannot pack the rest of my things until my trunk is delivered to my room." She said it like the spoiled, petulant child she once was.

Isaac smiled lightly and Emily knew he'd taken her meaning. He looked around the table of men and gestured helplessly. "I am correctly chastised for overlooking a woman's luggage. I'll have it delivered promptly."

"Thank you." She gave a toss of her hair.

Ezekiel appeared. He set a plate before her and filled her cup from a cut glass pitcher. When he had gone, Mr. Burrows asked, "So you are leaving, Miss Preston?"

Emily took up her fork. Her insides felt so queasy she didn't know if she could swallow. "Very soon."

"You won't even stay for this wedding Isaac has been telling me about?"

She paused a bit guiltily. "I've been away so long already."

Mr. Burrows turned to Isaac. "You know, a man with your name and background would have had the ladies scheming for his hand long ago in Carolina."

"A poor man, however, must rely more heavily on character," Isaac replied.

As Mr. Burrows pondered this, Emily wondered again how her uncle had lost his fortune, but she kept up her act. "I'm going to marry the richest man in Charleston County when I get home," she announced.

Mr. Burrows laughed out loud. "Spoken like a true

Southern belle!"

Isaac raised a skeptical eyebrow. "Aren't you still a bit young?"

She ignored him. "He has to have lots of money and lots of slaves. And if a one of them tries to escape, I'll promptly send for you, Mr. Burrows."

Perhaps she'd gone a bit overboard. The old Quaker couple had never been back, but she glanced around the dining room to make certain she hadn't upset anyone else. No one even sniffed. In fact, she'd been so late to the table the room was already beginning to empty.

She lowered her voice. "I have some information that may help you."

Her uncle looked up sharply, but she wouldn't even rat out Helen and Angelina. Her only thought was to send Mr. Burrows as far from the river as he would go. She cut her eyes at him craftily. "I had almost forgotten what I overheard at school this winter. Two of my classmates were whispering together about a fellow from Shyne's Grocery up on Charlotte Avenue who sometimes makes special afterhours deliveries. I wondered later just exactly what it was he delivered."

Mr. Burrows exchanged shrewd glances with his friends. He pushed his plate away and stood, his polished smile in place once again. "Miss Preston, I thank you. You have been very helpful. Isaac," he nodded, "always a pleasure."

With a flick of Mr. Burrows' head, his two lackeys followed him upstairs. Isaac winked at Emily before he also excused himself. When they were gone, she sank into her chair and worked to calm the elephants stampeding just beneath her ribs.

141

Chapter Eighteen

That afternoon Emily attempted some knitting—Julia had taught her how to make socks—just to maintain a sense of normalcy, but her hands shook so badly that she had to undo as many stitches as she created. She tried homework and painting and even opened her mother's book of poetry. Finally she gave up and took a walk.

The air was warm and the sun shone brightly as Emily twisted between high buildings. Ordinarily she would admire the fine architecture, the intricate cresting and carved cornices, but today she just felt closed in. She saw eyes at every window—curious eyes that watched to see where she would go, what she would do, who she would meet.

She hadn't seen Malachi since noon, nor had her uncle returned. She wished someone would tell her what was going on. Unable to wait any longer, she sought them out. Slipping into the alley beside the barn, she found the door and stepped inside.

She peered into the gloom that deepened as the sun sank behind the skyline. "Malachi?"

"I'm here," he answered. He was bent over a bundle. There was no sign of the runaways.

She closed the door and could hardly see. "What's going on? What do we do?"

Malachi straightened. "We wait for your uncle."

Emily's eyes were beginning to adjust to the dimness. "Where are they?"

"Who?"

"You know who!"

"Abraham and Rachel. They all have names." He gestured toward the hay. "They're sleeping."

Emily glanced around the barn. It looked the same, still smelled of hay and musty timbers, still housed the horrid wagon, but it had changed. Now it housed a secret, like the desk in her uncle's office. And even though it was hundreds, maybe a thousand miles from Southern plantations, two slaves had found their way to it.

"How'd they get here?" Emily asked. "Here, to this very spot, to you?"

"It's a station."

"A what?"

"A safe house on the Underground Railroad."

She had heard the term before, in a whispered phrase that had fallen dead when she approached the slave cabin. And she'd heard it uttered with anger and derision by the overseer of a neighboring plantation. But her father never spoke about such things.

"It's the *last* station," he continued, "and operated with signs and codes so you never would have known it was here if you hadn't stumbled inside."

They heard a soft rustle. "Can I see them?" she asked.

He led her to the back of the barn. It had grown quite dark. The black children were curled under their blanket, nestled into the back side of the haystack. Abraham slept, but Rachel fastened her eyes on them.

Emily approached tentatively. "Hello."

The girl remained motionless.

"Do they speak English?" Emily whispered.

Malachi nodded.

"Then why doesn't she respond?"

"You probably sound like her mistress. Rachel, this is my friend, Emily."

Rachel's eyes flickered. "You dress like Ol' Miss too."

Emily looked down at her favorite gown. She had forgotten to change out of it after dinner. She smiled gently at the girl. "But I'm not your mistress."

Rachel eyed Emily distrustfully. "You a fine lady, miss. You gots slaves, too?"

The question startled Emily. "My father—uh, yes, I suppose I do." Her face blazed in the dark barn.

"Why you helpin' us?"

Emily grew more flustered. She glanced down at the bandage on the girl's leg, at the blood.

Rachel sensed her discomfort and lifted a defiant chin. "Don't none of yo' people like bein' yo' slave."

In the same situation, Emily wondered if she would be as fearless as Rachel. "How did you dare to run in the face of such horrible penalties?" she asked.

"It take more courage to stay. Marse, he wanna make more slave babies."

Emily felt her throat constrict.

"We should redress that wound," Malachi announced, and stood to find the materials.

The blood looked black in the gloom. "What happened to your leg?" Emily asked.

"Hound two nights past. Abraham club it wid a stick. Ain't kilt though."

It hadn't killed the dog. Emily had seen both bloodhounds that afternoon, one sporting a thick bandage. They had accompanied the slave catchers. She hoped they were far north.

Malachi returned and carefully removed the old dressing from Rachel's leg. He smeared on a smelly salve and wrapped it snugly in a new length of cloth. Then he stood.

"It's just about time. Mr. deBaptiste's steamship is docked at the river and will be leaving in about two hours. These two need to be on it, along with some others I know of, but Burrows complicates things. If he's poking around, I'll lay a false trail and lead him out of town."

"How?"

"I'll swap clothing with Abraham. Tie some to my feet to leave the scent."

"Will that fool a bloodhound?"

"They'll smell it. Don't know if they'll follow it, but I have to try."

"What will I do?"

Malachi was quiet a long time. "I was going to ask you to come with me, but I spoke hastily this afternoon. It's not a good idea."

Emily bristled. "Why not?"

"Because—" he looked her up and down. "Because it's not safe," he finished lamely.

He didn't think she could do it, she realized, just like he hadn't thought she could muck out the barn. Her eyes flashed. "Malachi Watson, you think I can't keep up with you? That I'm not brave enough?"

He looked at the wall, and at the hay, but not at her.

"I'm going!" she exclaimed hotly, and she began tugging at the sash on her dress.

He scowled, "Emily, you don't know what you're getting into."

She started on the buttons.

"Your uncle will never let you."

She fixed him with a wicked glare, and he could see the battle was lost. With a sigh of resignation, he woke Abraham and they shambled to the other end of the barn.

As she gloated, Emily suddenly remembered the fine material under her fingers. She hesitated, caressing her beautiful gown.

Beside her, Rachel made an I-thought-so kind of noise. Emily locked eyes with her and shimmied out of the dress.

The slave girl quickly removed her own shift and stepped into Emily's pantalettes, petticoat, and gown and stood with her brown feet sticking out the bottom.

Emily looked regretfully at her shoes, tossed in the hay.

"Keep 'em," Rachel told her. "You need 'em more'n I do."

When they stepped from behind the hay, Abraham's eyes grew round. "Rachel, you's a fine lady!"

The girl shyly spread out the smooth fabric.

Malachi handed them each a bundle. Emily couldn't be sure, but they appeared to be wrapped in familiar gray cloth and tied with shapeless, knitted mufflers.

Just then, the big door slid open to reveal the silhouettes of Isaac and both horses.

"Where's Burrows?" Malachi whispered.

Emily could hear her uncle hitching the team to the wagon. "He left on a wild goose chase, but he's back already and mad as all get out. You ready?"

"Yes."

"We should have found someone to trade with the girl. Two would be better."

Malachi opened his mouth, but Emily silenced him with a shake of her head. "Her name is Rachel," he said instead.

"Well, get her and her brother under the tarp, and cover yourself as well. I'll drop you first. When I get there, I'll stop the wagon for a five count. If you head due east, the hounds can't help but cross you on their way to the river. I'll wait for you in the old Beubien barn."

The wagon bed was already arranged with a pile of hay. Several lumpy sacks sat off to one side, along with a few tools and a huge crosscut saw. The tarp was draped haphazardly across the back and partially covered with the hay. Isaac never even looked back as they scampered under it.

Emily scrunched up as small as she could make herself. Abraham's knee was in her back and the heavy canvas fabric stunk like mildew, but she hardly noticed. Her heart finally realized what her body was about to do and began to thunder in protest.

She heard a sprinkling of hay scatter over the top of the tarp, then the wagon swayed as Isaac climbed up and clucked to the horses. And with a lurch, Emily embarked on the most terrifying night of her life.

Chapter Nineteen

They'd hardly started when a booming voice hailed them. "Milford!"

Emily recognized Mr. Thatcher at once. She willed her uncle to drive on past, but he pulled up the horses and addressed the mill owner. "Hello, William. What's going on?"

"Nothing, nothing. Just on my way to a card game. But I ran into Burrows near your place. He's looking for a couple runaway kids. Told me to keep my eyes open."

"Sure. He told me, too."

"He's a good man, that Burrows. There ought to be stiffer penalties for helping slaves sneak through here. What'cha got in the wagon?"

Emily gulped and prayed the others would remain still.

"Not much. John Harrison couldn't meet the steamer today so I picked up his order, but I wasn't about to deliver that saw on horseback."

Mr. Thatcher guffawed loudly.

"I'll keep a look out for anything suspicious," Isaac promised and slapped the lines on the horses.

Emily dared to breathe again, and too soon the wagon jerked to another stop. Malachi tapped her knee and shimmied over the edge of the wagon bed. She followed as quickly as she could. Her uncle kept his eyes to the front as if, by not looking, he could protect them from other unwelcome glances.

Emily met Rachel's eyes as she dropped to the ground. "Good luck," she whispered as the wagon started up again. She took a steadying breath and caught sight of Malachi waving her into a dark doorway.

"What's that?" he asked, pointing to the strip of linen in her hand.

She held it up. Her hand was shaking. "Rachel's bandage." She hastily tied it around one of her shoes, praying it would fool the hounds yet hoping it would not.

Her teeth began to chatter. The night was mild, but her shift was short and thin and her legs were bare. "What do we do now?"

"Follow me. Stay in the shadows as much as possible and move quickly. The pickup point is a few miles off."

"What happens if Burrows finds us?"

"We run faster. Come on!"

They fled between buildings that looked far less forbidding by the light of day. The darkness felt heavy, and the occasional passerby turned to watch them flee. But the road was smooth and straight, and they covered ground quickly. After they crossed the railroad track the buildings began to thin out.

The land broadened and the road narrowed, becoming muddy and rutted as they passed between farms. Emily tripped and slid, glancing behind, gasping for breath. She had never raced this far, and she was thankful now for all the hard work that had made her muscles strong and taut.

Finally Malachi slowed. "We should have some time before Burrows finds our trail. Let's catch our breath."

They didn't stop but hustled along at something less than a run. Soon Emily's breathing regulated enough to ask a question Rachel had prompted. "Malachi, if our slaves at

Ella Wood really hate it there, like Rachel said, why do you suppose Zeke stayed after Uncle Isaac freed him?"

"Zeke *chose* to follow your mother. That's an important distinction."

"But if he was free, why not go do what he wanted?"

"Think about it, Emily. Slavery was all he'd ever known. He was an old man when your uncle freed him. How many choices were open to him?"

She changed the subject. "How far do we have to go?"

"Straight along this road, then cut over to the river. We're probably nearing halfway."

"Good." She jogged along, feeling more at ease. "I watched you change Rachel's bandage. I think you'll make a fine doctor."

He smiled. "And I think—"

A distant baying cut him off and tightened his smile. Fear dumped itself into Emily's gut like it was poured from a pail.

"Let's go!"

Malachi rocketed down the road, and Emily struggled to keep her feet under her in the mud. She watched Malachi nearly go down in front of her. A moment later, he clambered over the rail fence alongside the road. "The field is flatter," he said, helping her over.

They struggled through a meadow choked with last year's growth and picked up speed over a hayfield. They passed through field after field, tearing through briars, sliding through mud, pushing through woods, flitting from tree to tree, dark and silent as black moonbeams. Emily's legs burned and her breath came in great, gulping pants, but the memory of Rachel's slashed leg kept her pounding ahead of the dogs, hoping Malachi knew where he was going.

The sound of baying grew steadily louder behind them.

"This way!" Malachi veered off the road and splashed

150

into a small creek. "Maybe they'll lose our trail in the water."

The creek wasn't deep, but the bottom was uneven, and it splattered all the way up Emily's thigh. She clenched her teeth against water still as cold as winter's breath.

They followed the creek under a fence and through a field of cows. Startled from their warm spring beds, the cows lunged to their feet and ran lowing across the field.

In the open space, the stars unrolled across the sky: the scorpion, Hercules, and the great dipper all in their familiar places. And above them all, the North Star was the hinge that held them in position.

The North Star! The Candle Star, guiding them, showing the way! Now she knew Malachi was indeed holding them to their direction. They were headed east.

The creek rounded a bend and flowed beneath a canopy of trees. By this time Emily's feet had gone quite numb, and in the dark she tripped over a fallen log and fell headlong into the water.

She came up spluttering and shivering, choking on the water streaming down her face. Malachi dragged her out of the creek and up the bank and set her down in a patch of grass.

"Are you okay?"

She nodded, unable to speak through her chattering teeth.

"Emily, I'm sorry. I never should have let you come. It was foolish of me." He smacked his fist on his knee in frustration and anger. "I sure wish you hadn't stumbled through that barn door this afternoon!"

Emily was regretting that too, but there was nothing to do now but keep moving. She raised herself to her feet, shivering violently.

"M-Malachi," she chattered, "what will happen if w-we're caught?"

151

"You will return home, to your parents' embarrassment."

"And you?"

He shrugged.

"You'd g-go to jail, wouldn't you?"

"If I'm lucky."

She gasped, suddenly realizing the cost of Malachi's gamble. "You could be taken as a slave!"

"Mr. Milford would never allow that." But his voice was strained.

"W-what if he didn't know?" Why had she insisted on coming along? She was only slowing him down.

"Come on, we still have a lot of ground to cover. And take that rag off your foot!"

She saw he had already discarded his. She yanked the bandage loose and tucked it inside her shift.

She could hear the dogs getting closer and closer. She saw again a vision of the bloody slash on Rachel's leg, and she ran. Over fields and fences and streams, wondering just how far they had traveled.

She ran like a stalked creature. She thought of the stories her brother told of hunting in the woods back home, of how raccoons could outwit a dog. Sometimes they would escape by climbing above the reach of a dog's nose and traveling tree to tree like a squirrel. Other times they might run along a fence rail and drop back to the ground far from the point they climbed up. They would even double back. They were wily creatures, raccoons.

Just then they broke out of a glade of trees. Moonlight bathed the field beyond, illuminating a barn at the far end. A barn with an odd silhouette. With a jolt, Emily recognized it.

"Malachi, is this where we came for the state fair last fall?" she panted.

"I think so. Yeah. I see the platform on top of the barn

where that fellow in the glider rolled off."

Her heart leaped. "Come on, I have an idea!"

She raced toward the barn, hoping the tall platform meant the heavy guy wires were still there, supporting the structure, stretching fifty yards beyond the barn.

They were! She almost tripped on one as they approached.

Malachi hesitated. "If we go in the barn, we're sitting ducks."

"Not in the barn, *on* it," she corrected. "Climb!"

"I hope you know what you're doing," he mumbled as they grabbed hold of the scaffolding and began pulling themselves up.

It didn't take long. From the top of the platform they could look out over the surrounding fields. The river sparkled not far away.

"Look!" Malachi exclaimed in a loud whisper. "The dogs!"

The baying was loud and clear now. Both animals could be seen only a quarter of a mile away.

Emily found where the guy wires attached to the scaffolding. She grabbed hold of the thick cable, swung her legs around, and started shimmying down.

"Are you crazy? What are you doing?" Malachi hissed.

"I'm being a raccoon."

"You're what?"

"If we can fool Burrows' hounds into thinking we're in the barn, it will take some time for the men to come up and realize we're not."

Malachi sucked in his breath and quickly latched onto the cable behind her. Before the dogs came galloping across the barnyard, the children were racing through the trees on the far side.

The hounds set up a racket inside the barn, and Emily and Malachi hugged each other joyfully.

153

"How far?" Emily whispered.

"Just down the road and to the river. We're almost there."

"Good. I'm about played out."

Seven minutes later, a rickety barn loomed up in the darkness. They could still hear the hounds baying in the distance. Malachi called out, and Isaac drove out of the barn. "Get in."

They wasted no time. Isaac slapped the reins and the team took off down the road. After a safe distance, Isaac pulled over. They were on a bulge of land that jutted out slightly into the river, and they had a good view of the water rolling back in either direction. Lights in Canada twinkled across the expanse of black velvet water, and Belle Isle sprawled low in front of them.

Isaac turned to them, his voice tight. "Emily, when I saw that child get out of the wagon in your dress—" his voice caught. "What were you thinking, girl?"

She lifted her chin defiantly. "Can't you guess? You're the one who told me we're just alike."

After a tense moment, Isaac's chuckle dropped softly around them. "Fool girl," he muttered. "I ought to take a hickory stick to your backside. When we get home, you scoot in that house and change, and don't you dare tell Shannon what you've been up to. She'd fillet us both."

Malachi jumped out of the wagon, squinting downriver, and Emily let the silence run on. Finally she spoke. "I don't think Shannon would care."

"What do you mean by that?"

Emily shifted uncomfortably on the seat. "I've been pretty awful to her."

Isaac pursed his lips and nodded. "Yes, you have. But she loves you. Give her a chance."

Malachi's shout broke the moment. "There! Do you see it?"

"See what?" Emily craned her neck.

"The lights on the steamer. It's moving out into the river."

"I see it!"

"They made it! They're all safe!"

"How can you tell?"

"See the red light up on top of the ship? That's the signal that everyone is accounted for. Mr. deBaptiste will cross to Canada before heading down to Cleveland."

They watched the lights on the ship grow smaller. Then Isaac twitched the reins. "Let's get on home. I intend to be sitting in my office when Burrows comes in the door madder than a bear with consumption."

Chapter Twenty

Emily waited at the foot of the hotel steps, wearing her second-best gown and holding a tremendous bouquet of roses. Shannon's sister stood beside her, and the lobby swarmed with red-haired nieces and nephews mixed in among the dark faces of Julia, Malachi, and Zeke.

Dressed in his best suit with his riot of curls neatly combed, Isaac sat at the piano. He played once through an old hymn, and as he moved smoothly into "Moonlight Sontata," the bride appeared at the top of the stairs. She floated down to the beautiful melody, eyes shining, hair falling in ringlets onto a soft blue gown. Isaac couldn't take his eyes off her.

Shannon had been overjoyed when Emily finally pruned off the last of her pride and abolished the uneasy truce. Then it hadn't taken much effort for the young woman to talk Emily into staying for the wedding.

After the ceremony they would feast on Julia's delicious cooking, and that afternoon Emily's train would leave for home. But for now Emily stood contentedly within the circle of her patchwork family, blooming like the roses in Shannon's garden.

***

Emily changed into her new traveling suit and laid one last petticoat on the pile overflowing the top of her trunk. She couldn't imagine how she was going to close the lid. Why was it that on returning a trunk always seemed smaller?

Only a few items remained on her bed, and most of these she shoved into her handbag. That left only a stained strip of white linen—Rachel's bandage.

The cloth had been laundered, and now Emily rolled it into a tight ball and shoved it into a corner of her trunk. It would serve as a reminder to look for "little things" on the plantation. She did not want to forget the color of blood.

A knock sounded at the door and Isaac peeked in. "Almost ready?"

She nodded. "But it will take a miracle to latch this trunk."

"You don't weigh enough," he told her. "Allow me."

He sat on the lid. It closed with a groan and she fastened the lock.

"Now let's pray the catch doesn't spring open and litter the compartment with ladies' undergarments," he joked.

She laughed, thinking such a scene could be entertaining on the long train ride.

"If you're all set, there's something I'd like to show you before you leave."

Emily gave the latch one final inspection before following him into his office. The top of the Dutch door was firmly closed.

Isaac sat at his desk and pressed a small panel. The secret compartment popped open, and he removed the journal with the star embossed on its cover.

"Only Julia, Shannon, and Malachi know the contents of this book, but as the newest conductor at this station, and as my most trusted niece—"

"I'm your only niece."

"Not anymore," he grinned.

"—descended from the same dubious lineage, the niece most like me in thought and temperament, I assumed you might like to know exactly where the Milford family fortune went."

He opened the journal to a random page and held it open for her to see. Dated March 14, 1855, it looked just like all the other entries she remembered. She read through the list, "Joe, Solomon, six sacks of apples, three hundred pounds seed corn, three plows, twenty spades, twenty hoes, woolen cloth, fourteen buckets."

The next entry, dated two weeks later, looked much the same. "Anna, Thomas, Daniel, five lanterns, fifteen gallons kerosene, oxen yoke."

Emily took the book and thumbed through several more pages. Some entries had names and no items, others listed just materials, but still she could make no sense of the notations.

"You still don't understand?" He turned to the very last entry. Dated a few weeks before, it read, "Rachel, Abraham, four axes, ten hammers, one crosscut saw, twenty sacks feed."

The light finally dawned. Emily flipped to the beginning. It was dated fifteen years before. She gawked at her uncle. "Is this why you moved to the North?"

He nodded. "I had an uncle who was very wise. He saw what I was becoming and offered to take me under his wing for a time. My father readily agreed. So I spent two tough years learning to work and gaining a new perspective on life.

"It was my uncle who first introduced me to the Underground Railroad. Together we helped more than forty runaways pass right under my father's nose.

"When my parents died I inherited the estate, and my

first act as the new master was to free every slave. Then I sold out. Of course, much of the value of the estate was in slaves, and my father had several creditors. So most folks, including your father, assumed I was foolish and broke."

"But you had enough to buy this hotel," Emily figured.

"And some left over, which I have put to use outfitting former slaves when they settle in Canada. With the help of many individuals, both black and white, supplies are collected and transported across the river."

"And you did this while Mr. Burrows boarded in your house?"

Isaac laughed. "He'd be proud to know how many black families he's financed!"

"Does my mama know what you're doing up here?"

He smiled gently. "Do you think she would have let you come? No, she thinks I'm a misplaced Southern gentleman with no eye for business, but she did recognize the changes wrought by my uncle's hand. And I think she'll be very proud of you."

He closed the book and replaced it in its hiding place. "I'll see to your trunk."

***

Emily sat in the window seat and faced the cinnamon-colored depot. She had exchanged a dozen final hugs, accepted a huge basket of food from Julia, and promised Malachi she would send for his books immediately. Then Isaac slipped her a parcel wrapped in brown paper. "Just a little something to remember us by," he winked.

The train let out a sharp whistle and lurched into motion like a beast awakened from slumber. Emily waved to her family until the train inched around the curve and the waterfront was lost to sight.

As the train picked up speed, Emily opened her gift.

159

Inside she found a small book of Longfellow's poetry. She laughed out loud and held the volume up for Zeke to see. But the old man had already fallen asleep, his gray hair resting against the back of his seat, his mouth open slightly.

Emily smiled fondly at him and lost herself in the beauty of cadence and rhyme.

Keep reading to sort fact from fiction and
catch a sneak peek at the next book in the collection.

Emily's story continues...

Charleston, South Carolina, 1860

As slavery pushes the nation toward war, Emily must battle her father in her own bid for freedom. She's prepared to pay any price to escape the plantation and attend a northern university newly opened to women. Meanwhile Thaddeus Black, her handsome and unwanted suitor, simply won't take no for an answer. While her mind is willing to strike out alone, her heart stubbornly refuses to accept that a choice for independence must be a choice against love. 14+ age recommendation

Book one is FREE at
www.michelleisenhoff.

Historical Note

Sometimes when writing historical fiction, the line between truth and imagination blurs. I'd like to take the opportunity to identify some factual people and events mentioned in *The Candle Star*.

Michigan played a very important role in the Underground Railroad, the network of secret routes escaping slaves followed to Canada. Seven lines crossed the state, most running through Detroit. My inspiration for *The Candle Star* came from the true account of a Detroit man named Seymour Finney who hid runaways in his barn while hosting slave catchers in his hotel. The railroad stock advertisement Zeke read was taken from an 1853 Detroit UGRR broadside now kept by the Detroit Public Library.

The most important historical figure to appear in my story was Frederick Douglass. A former slave, he rose to become one of the most eloquent and influential American orators of his day. He really did speak in the Second Baptist Church of Detroit on March 12, 1859. There is no record of what he said that day. The words I have written for him are actually his own, taken from several of his speeches then lumped into one address and shaped to fit this story.

George deBaptiste was another real-life character. His steamship, the *T. Whitney*, frequently carried human cargo to safety. Mr. deBaptiste hosted Frederick Douglass in his home where he met with the famous abolitionist, John Brown, after the address at Second Baptist. Malachi's friends Mr. William Lambert and Dr. Joseph Ferguson, both noted Detroit abolitionists, were also in attendance and also members of Second Baptist. The church, the first in Michigan to be started by free Blacks, was instrumental in assisting thousands of runaway slaves to freedom. It still operates in Detroit today.

Sir George Cayley, an engineer from Scarborough, England, was the first person to discover the principles of flight. In 1853, he built and successfully tested the first manned glider. It probably wasn't recreated and demonstrated five years later at an American state fair, but it could have been. All the other inventions mentioned at the fair were also accurate to the time period. Flying Tom Landless is fictional.

Henry Wadsworth Longfellow was one of America's most noteworthy poets. He was alive and very popular when this story takes place. The quotes are taken from his poems "Autumn," "The Building of the Ship," and "To the River Charles" in that order.

Finally, *Uncle Tom's Cabin*, the book mentioned by Emily in chapter three, was published by Harriet Beecher Stowe in 1852 and helped to popularize the abolitionist movement, which aided the nomination of Abraham Lincoln to the presidency, which in turn led to the Civil War in 1861.

Visit Michelle's website for a variety of
FREE BOOKS.

www.michelleisenhoff.com

Enjoy this sneak peek into book two,
BLOOD OF PIONEERS

Chapter One

Wayland, Michigan, 1862

One honest glimpse of freedom has the power to twist life into a coyote trap. Routines that once gave Hannah Wallace a measure of contentment now ensnared her, dulling her imagination, chaining her painfully in place. In contrast, her brother bounded down the street like a rabbit freed from a cage.

Hannah watched him with a mingling of jealousy and pride. He looked dashing in his Sunday best, buttons gleaming, hat set at a rakish angle, newly shined boots kicking up puffs of dust. He was young, handsome, confident, and off to save the Union. Oh, what she wouldn't give to be leaving town with him!

Seth had only been seventeen when fighting first broke out, not old enough to join up without lying like his friend Jamison Coops had done. Folks signed up in droves, afraid the war would end before they had a chance to make a name for themselves. Seth had begged and pleaded, cried and even swore, but Pa stood firm. War was dirt and illness and sweat and killing, and no underage boy of his was going to participate. Pa's pessimism didn't dampen Seth's enthusiasm any, but his sharp eye did keep him from sneaking off, so the boy had to wait.

Then early this summer the recruiters came back. Soon as Seth heard, he let out a whoop, dropped his pitchfork, and lit out for town. Hannah tagged along, positively green with envy, and watched him set his name down with a flourish. His lopsided grin sparkled with charm and innocence. "With a Wallace man in the mix," he boasted, "the war will be over in no time."

"That's the spirit!" the recruiter encouraged. After a year of fighting, volunteers had grown scarce. Returning veterans advertised the destruction of warfare too well. The dead spoke even louder. "I wish I had ten thousand more boys like you, son."

"Won't need 'em, sir." Seth swelled with pride and confidence. "I'll lick those Rebs myself. All the way back to Richmond."

Richmond! How Hannah would love to see it. Washington, too. And Charleston and Montgomery and the mountains and the ocean and all the other places the newspaper filled itself with nowadays. They sounded so far away—exotic and exciting. And her crummy brother would probably get to see them all.

She watched as Seth joined the gathering in the park square. A dozen recruits from the farms round about sat in the grass and on old stumps, rendezvousing for the first leg of their journey, the county seat in Allegan. Hannah knew many of them. Their number included a few older men, but most were young, raw-boned farmers leaving home for the first time.

Her eyes flicked immediately to Walter Beasley, whose wrists poked a good three inches beyond his cuffs. He had sprouted up faster than a new row of corn, and his poor mama never could keep up. But his smile was open and friendly, and Hannah had always liked him.

Next to Walter stood cocky little Tommy Stockdale,

the blacksmith's son and her own brother-in-law, with his bellyful of wild stories and a penchant for thinking up ideas fool enough to land an entire Sunday school class in trouble. Her oldest sister, Maddy, had run off and married Tommy as soon as she turned sixteen. Mama and Pa didn't like the idea of her getting hitched so young, especially with a war on, but they figured stopping her would only push her into a peck of trouble, so they reluctantly agreed.

Walter slapped Seth on the back. "Glad you could join us, Wallace. Gunna need you for my rear guard. When they slap a uniform on this fine-tuned body, every girl from Wayland to Washington is going to come begging me to marry her."

"Sure," Seth jibed, "until you open your mouth and start talking."

Walter grinned.

"I'm sorry, gentlemen," Tommy informed them with mock dismay, "but the war will be over before we can even muster in. Someone leaked to the press that I was joining up, and the South entered into immediate peace negotiations."

The others moaned and rolled their eyes, and Tommy punched Seth on the arm good-naturedly. "What a time we're going to have, boys!" he whooped.

Hannah's attention was turned by someone calling her name. Wes Carver waved at her from across the street where he stood on a tree stump gawking at the new soldiers, plainly wishing he was among their number. His older brother had left several months before with a similar group of men. Since then his mother had discovered Wes drilling with a stolen kitchen broom more than once.

Hannah skipped over to join her schoolmate, passing between storefronts draped with red, white, and blue bunting. "Isn't this exciting?" she exclaimed.

"Sure! It's the only thing ever happens in this town.

But don't tell my father I said so." He dropped his voice with a nervous peek behind him. "I'd catch it good if he knew I was here. According to him, all those fellows are off to certain death or dismemberment."

Hannah brushed off the dire prediction. "There wouldn't be any glory without a little risk."

Of course war had casualties. Every week or so the *Allegan Record* published a list of county men who had died or been injured in the various conflicts. Hannah had known some of them, but tragedy hadn't touched her personally. Death, for the greater part, remained distant and faceless. Stories of gallantry and bravery in battle, however, had grown in the telling until even a plucky girl could imagine herself a hero. Old men might complain of the war's cost and its length, but not Hannah.

"Danger just adds to the romance," she concluded.

"Romance!" Wes spluttered as if the word tasted of quinine. "You girls sure have a way of turning everything into ribbons and daisies. War is about honor! The South has challenged the North, and we have to fight them."

"Oh, blast your honor," Hannah scoffed. "This isn't a gentlemen's duel. You and I both know the South is just a bunch of dirty rebels who chose to disregard the law and leave the Union. I wish I could be the one to teach them a lesson."

Wes bit back a devilish grin. He never could resist a provocation. "Aw, you're just a girl."

Hannah stamped her foot with a crunch of gravel. "John Wesley Carver! I can shoot the eye out of a squirrel at a hundred paces!"

He crossed his arms. "That don't mean nothing. You couldn't shoot a person."

Hannah missed the mischief in his eye. "I could so! They're nothing but stinking Rebs who need shooting, and if I can't do it, at least my brother can!" She could feel the

170

heat rising in her cheeks and knew it wasn't from the sticky August weather.

Wes straightened, suddenly serious. "Is that your pa joining up with the boys?"

Hannah had seen him, too, and some of the color faded from the banners. "What's it look like?" she snapped.

"Thought he didn't hold with fighting any more than my pa."

"He don't."

"Then why's he in there? The fellows rankle him too much?"

Hannah didn't answer. Pa had taken some ribbing off a few of the neighbors. They said his son was a braver man than he, but Hannah knew that wasn't why he signed his name. The real reason was to keep an eye on Seth and make sure he didn't "get his fool head blown off." She had heard him say as much to Mama that very morning as they lingered alone at the breakfast table.

"The wheat should pay off the debt, Amelia," he had said. "Right now our son needs me more than this farm does."

"It's not the farm I'm worried about, Henry."

Hannah had chosen that moment to barge into the room, causing her father to slosh his coffee. "It's not fair!" she cried.

Mama sighed. "Not you, too, child." Her eyes were red.

"You and Seth both get to go off and do something important, but I'll be stuck on this farm for the rest of my life. I wish I was a boy!"

Pa wiped his hand with a handkerchief then turned to face her. His voice was as rich and brown as soil. "First of all, you're only thirteen years old. Too young for war even if you were a boy. And second, you've just named two good reasons why you're needed here at home. With Seth and I both gone, your mama is going to need your help more than ever."

Hannah crossed her arms spitefully. "She's got Joel and Justin," she said, naming her older and younger brothers. "And Maddy's moving home, too. They can help her."

Pa stood and rested his hands on Hannah's shoulders. "It's noble of you to want to fight, honey, but the North is going to need a different kind of help from you. The Union will need what this farm can produce. How do you think the army gets its bread, its meat, its horses? You will be serving your country right here."

She had looked up at her father with tears brimming in her eyes, and it hadn't taken him long to discover the real reason for her outburst. "Aw, Peanut," he said, pulling her against him in a tight embrace. "I'll miss you, too. More than anything."

That made the tears overflow. "Don't go, Pa." It was one thing for Seth or Tommy to go seeking for adventure, but Pa? He belonged here with his family. Here with her.

Pa pulled her chin up and wiped her eyes with his sleeve. "I won't be gone forever, darling. I'll be home before you know it. And it will help me to know you're being brave."

She had promised. But now, watching her father join the others, her resolve felt as fragile as straw.

"Your pa should have stayed home." Wes frowned. "He's thirty-nine, for crying out loud. My brother says the old ones are the first to get sick."

Tears burned Hannah's eyes. "Shut up, Wes Carver! You don't know anything!" She punched him hard and flew across the fields toward home as her father took his first step down the long, long road to Allegan.

172

Also by Michelle Isenhoff

The Mountain Trilogy:
(middle grade Oriental fantasy)
*Semi-finalist in the 2013 Kindle Book Review book
awards* (Song of the Mountain).

Taylor Davis Series:
(middle grade humorous sci-fi/adventure)
*Finalist for the 2015 kid-judged Wishing Shelf Inde-
pendent Book Award* (Flame of Findul).

The Quill Pen:
(middle grade historical fiction with some magic)
Awarded a Readers' Favorite 5 Star Seal.

Recompense Series:
(best-selling young adult sci-fi)
*Reader-nominated for the 2018 Cybils
Award* (Recompense).

MICHELLE ISENHOFF's work has been reader-nominated for a Cybils Award, the Great Michigan Read, and the Maine Student Book Award. She's also placed as a semi-finalist in the Kindle Book Review Book Awards, a finalist in the Wishing Shelf Book Awards, and earned multiple Readers' Favorite 5 Star seals of approval. A former teacher and longtime homeschooler, Michelle has written extensively in the children's genre and been lauded by the education community for the literary quality of her work. These days, she writes full time in the adult historical fiction and speculative fiction genres. To keep up with her new books, sign up at http://hyperurl.co/new-release-list.

Made in the USA
San Bernardino, CA
03 June 2019